I picked up this book and didn't want to put it down - Jerry is an excellent storyteller. His book is packed with extremely important and insightful material.

A must read for people already involved in democratic education, for those thinking of getting into it, or for those who just want to learn about it.

If it were up to me I'd make this mandatory reading for every parent and every educator. Simple and profound!

Roger Dennis
Public School teacher

Finally, the one book you need in order to know everything there is to be known about kids and schooling. Told in simple, straightforward language, this eminently readable, admirably short book has finally been published!

The contents are drawn from numerous talks made by Jerry after many years of dedicated work running his school, publishing an almanac and a newsletter to help families, teachers and kids locate schools for themselves, visiting schools and attending conferences all over the world.

This is unquestionably THE BOOK for families and kids who want to get right down to the rock bottom truths that all kids know about learning - and "learning" in school! Too many people with too many vested interests have been fudging it or obscuring it for much too long! Read it from cover to cover!

Mary Leue
Founder: Albany Free School, SKOLE,
Paths of Learning, Journal of Family Life

As one who has experienced democracy in education first hand, I feel Jerry's book gives an accurate and honest depiction of how democracy can and does work in education. This is a truly wonderful book that I will suggest to people over and over again.

Isaac Graves
16-year-old homeschooler and alumnus of
the Albany Free School

No Homework
and
Recess All Day

How To Have
Freedom and Democracy
In Education

Jerry Mintz

BRAVURA Books

I'd like to greatfully acknowledge the contribution of three people who helped me put this book together:

Albert Lamb, for organizing the material and doing the editing,

Dana Bennis, for conducting the many interviews on which it is based,

Carol Morley, for tirelessly working on all the transcriptions.

Many thanks.

Jerry

You can contact Jerry Mintz at

AERO

(Alternative Education Resource Organization)
471 Roslyn Rd., Roslyn Heights, NY
(516) 621-2195
JerryAERO@aol.com
www.educationrevolution.org

BRAVURA Books

Printed in the United States of America
Book design and illustration by Albert Lamb

Contents

Forward

by Ron Miller

In this refreshing and enchanting book about democratic education, Jerry Mintz tells us that he is not a historian. Having known and worked with him for the last seventeen years, I can readily explain why: As the most dynamic, tireless activist and networker in the world of educational alternatives, he's far too busy challenging the present educational situation and shaping the future to spend much time dwelling on the past. Jerry is certainly familiar enough with the origins of diverse alternative approaches and understands where they fit on the complex map of modern education, but the great value of his work— and of this book—comes from his stories of young people's compelling experiences of freedom, community, and authentic learning that he has been either facilitating or observing for nearly forty years.

Like the eloquent advocates of educational freedom who have inspired so many of us in this movement—John Holt, A.S. Neill, George Dennison and their peers—Jerry speaks in plain, common-sense language about the meaning of *democracy.* Very simply, he says, democracy means that people have the power to "make real decisions about their lives." If we would let it, this fundamental principle can cut through all the ideological bickering between liberals and conservatives, humanists and those of religious faith, and most of the other moral and cultural identifications that divide us from each other. As this book clearly illustrates, democracy is not a formal set of beliefs or rules, but a flexible, generous spirit of community that enables people to work together to meet their various needs and achieve their diverse aspirations. Who can argue against that? Why would we send our children to schools that violate such an elemental and sacred principle?

Jerry has spent years interacting with small groups of people—in schools, homeschooling groups, and other local, voluntary associations—and knows how a genuine community forms and how to effectively keep one alive and thriving. In this book, he tells delightful stories about some of these places and shows what lessons he has drawn from his extensive experiences. Since *I'm* the historian here, I should tell you that the democratic schools Jerry describes are excellent examples of the voluntary associations that Alexis de Tocqueville, in the landmark study *Democracy in America* that he wrote in the mid-nineteenth century, proclaimed to be essential to the survival and health of a democratic culture. One does not need to be an anarchist to appreciate the value of Tocqueville's insight that when power becomes too highly concentrated (in either public or private institutions), people lose their sense of belonging to a community where their interests or their individuality truly matter. Many other writers and social scientists have emphasized this point, but their wisdom has had little influence on our rapidly globalizing society and virtually none on our increasingly standardized and authoritarian schools. This book takes us back to that wisdom.

Democratic education challenges not only the sterile anonymity and conformity of conventional schooling, but also its assumptions about the process of learning itself. Jerry's profession of confidence in the child's innate ability and desire to learn is a fundamental principle for alternative educators. This confidence does not come from an abstract theory of human development but from the experience of seeing hundreds and hundreds of young people make sense of their lives, as well as impressive leaps in their understanding and knowledge of the world, when they are allowed to learn what is interesting, relevant, and meaningful to them. In the pages that follow, you will see that education really can be a natural unfolding of our potentials, an exciting human adventure, which does not need the tight grip of management, measurement, and control that conventional schooling has applied to it.

Is this book, then, the last word on education? Well, no. I think there is more to the art of teaching than many "democratic" educators acknowledge; Jerry's brief criticism of Rudolf Steiner's and John Dewey's philosophies, for example, brushes aside their often sophisticated and important ideas about teaching, learning, democracy, and the nature of the human being. Personally, I don't think that "freedom" is the all-purpose answer to every educational question. But from where we stand in the world today, facing an overwhelming concentration of power and authority in massive impersonal institutions, the democratic educator's passion for freedom and community is a vitally important impulse that we should honor and nurture. We need more freedom, not less—an observation that this little book convincingly demonstrates.

Ron Miller, Ph.D., is the author of *Free Schools, Free People: Education and Democracy After the 1960s*. He is on the faculty of the Teacher Education program at Goddard College, Jerry Mintz's *alma mater*.

I hate this darn unthinking school
Which professes to teach you the Golden Rule -
"You fool me and I'll make you a fool"
Against this I will rebel

Many's the time when I've hated to stay
When the bored, boring teacher had nothing to say.
But "No!" says the teacher, "You can't go away!"
And this I will also retell

So I learned what the bored, boring teacher had
taught
And, thusly, I learned to be bored on the spot.
And ever since, I've been bored at the thought
Of the trash that the school has to sell

Oh, I'm sure education in school's not all bad
And I'll know things of interest when I am a grad.
But the camouflage job on the interest is sad
And the learning won't set very well

And so every morning at just 9 o' clock
I rush in the school and behind me they lock
The door to my prison, and I start to walk
Through the prison, from cell to cell.

A poem by Jerry Mintz,
written when he was a 15 year old
high school student.

Chapter One
The Magic of Democracy

The word "democracy" is one of the most overused words these days, which tends to water down its meaning. But democracy should mean something very specific: the empowerment of a group of people to make real decisions about their lives—the ability for them to make a decision and have that be the thing that happens.

Of course, democracy in a school is problematic because we have compulsory school laws. This means that no matter how democratic a school is, there is still a compulsory aspect because kids have to be in some kind of a school or educational program. We assume that anybody who is in a democratic school is there because they want to be in that school as opposed to another school. That doesn't necessarily mean that they want to be there rather than doing something else.

But, given that caveat, democracy in a school works the same way as it does anywhere: when a decision needs to be made, it gets made by all the people in the school. This should also mean that when a decision about an individual needs to be made, the particular individual can make it about him- or herself as long as it doesn't have a direct impact on other people, in which case it has to be a community decision. This is why democratic schools were originally called "free" schools.

I am making an underlying assumption about this idea of giving democratic power to kids that I should put on the table right away. This assumption is that people are natural learners. Children are natural learners. They don't need to be "motivated" to learn. Really, we have no way of predicting what kinds of things each one of us is going to want to learn or going to want to do. In fact the words "learn" and "do" pretty much blur together—learning isn't in some separate compartment. Even if people are being forced to study something, you can never tell exactly what they are learning or when they're learning. We can make guesses, but we're not always right.

Because children are natural learners, children in a democratic school, who are a part of a democratic meeting, can tap into a source of energy and creativity that is not accessed in an ordinary school. People use words like "spontaneity" and "creativity" but you don't truly see those qualities in action except in a learning situation where anything is possible, where the kids aren't always being told what to do.

When I talk to kids about the school that I used to direct, a school called Shaker Mountain, it usually only takes them about ten seconds to understand the basic philosophy. I tell them that at our school all the decisions were made democratically and you didn't have to go to classes unless you wanted to. At that point, the kids will often do a double take and look at me and say, "You don't have to go to classes unless you want to? I want to go to that school!"

It's amazing how consistent that response is, and how many kids know that this is what they want. And it's also amazing how few adults will even acknowledge this reaction as meaningful. It often infuriates me how our culture accepts the idea that kids don't like school—it's almost a joke—though we know through modern brain research that the brain is aggressive and wants to learn and that kids are natural learners.

People think that if kids don't like school, maybe the kids are lazy. Maybe something is wrong with their school. Probably the biggest revolution that could take place in schools all across the country would simply be to open the classroom door—to have classes be optional—and to have worthwhile places for the kids to go if they don't want to be in class.

This is already the case in a school called the School of Self-Determination, an inner-city public school with 1200 students. In this school, the students have been given a constitutional right to leave any class they want, without explanation. The decisions at this school are made by a democratic parliament. The students also interview the teachers before they are hired: the teachers get to do practice classes, and then the students vote on which teachers are going to be hired. And this school is in inner city Moscow, in Russia!

But we have to be careful. Democracy can't be faked. Children absolutely can tell when they're being given real power. It's interesting how quickly they know— within seconds.

This is one reason why democracy in a school is a fragile thing. Sometimes adults in a democratic school will overturn a decision that the students have made or ignore a decision of the school's meeting. When this happens the credibility of the meeting crumbles. No self-respecting kid is going to reinvest himself in that situation for a long while.

It's hard to communicate to people just what this democratic power is unless they've experienced it. I know that every place I've gone, when I do a demonstration of democratic process—and I always call it a demonstration—within five or ten minutes the process takes on a life of its own. You can feel the power of it as soon as people discover that they're talking about real and significant things and are in a position to make real and significant decisions. They sense the power of the ideas and of themselves.

Most schools don't give kids the opportunity to make decisions because the adults in them were systematically disempowered themselves, as children. They have come to fear making decisions and therefore don't believe that kids should be left to make decisions for themselves. Most adults have never, for the most part, experienced freedom, and therefore are afraid of it.

When people haven't experienced freedom they are afraid of what they might do if they had freedom. What people fear is, for example, some of the anger coming out that has built up in themselves over a period of time. And that is scary. If they haven't come through to the other side of these feelings they just don't know what it will be like after they become a free person. So it can be hard for them to believe that kids have the ability to live in freedom.

In the 1960s, when William Golding's book *The Lord of the Flies* came out, I was in upstate New York at a free, democratic school called Lewis-Wadhams. When we talked about this book with the kids who were at the school, they said, "Well, of course, those particular kids would become monsters if left alone on an island. They are English schoolboys and that's the way they would react. They've been in a very authoritarian system and therefore they would set up a hierarchy and have scapegoats. This would not happen if it were a group of kids from a school like this and we were shipwrecked there. We would know how to operate cooperatively." I even thought about writing a book called *Fellowship of the Flies* about such a situation.

It is not easy to make a leap of faith and trust children with power over their own lives, not having experienced it yourself. One of the main things I recommend to potential democratic schoolteachers, or to parents, is to see a democratic school in operation. You have to actually see the process happening and then you can, at least on an intellectual level, begin to see that it does work. Even after you have seen it with your own eyes, something on a gut level may still try to tell you that it's important to force kids to do things or they won't learn. But at least at that point you may have the intellectual ability to stop yourself and to begin to let the democratic process happen.

In a way it comes down almost to our most basic religious or philosophical belief systems: do we personally believe in original sin or in original goodness? I've had Christian fundamentalist home schoolers tell me that they could not do unschooling because of original sin. But if, as a founder of a school, you believe that children are naturally good and are natural learners, you may be open to the idea of democratic education.

At the heart of a democratic school is the democratic meeting, and a democratic meeting is more than the sum of its parts. When you get a group of people together and they are really making a decision and working on it together, a power is involved that seems to go well beyond what any administrator or group of teachers could decide. I sometimes feel frustrated when I talk to people who have very nice schools in which they meet the kids' needs and have a pleasant environment and fun things to do, but the kids don't actually make the basic decisions about their process in school meetings. I feel they have no idea what they're missing.

It's great when kids have nice teachers, are interested in the subjects that are being presented to them, aren't bored. But these kids don't have the same sense of being in control of their own educational process. They are becoming dependent on the adults, whom they feel are taking care of them so well, and that's a very different situation from kids who know that they are taking real responsibility for their own education.

It is even worse in public schools. Layers and layers of bureaucracy have built up over the years and ossified a system that was rigid to begin with. Every time some little thing goes wrong they invent yet another rule to make it even more difficult for people to do things. You can read what John Gatto has to say to discover whether the public school system was ever designed to be a freeing or democratizing institution. It certainly isn't one now.

As time goes on in public schools, as kids grow older, they inevitably become disempowered. When I talk about democracy in school, people ask me what seems to them a reasonable question: "What about younger kids? They can't handle democracy, can they?"

The fact is, younger kids have not been as disempowered as older kids and are far more capable of making good decisions and accepting the full responsibility of making those decisions. It seems quite reasonable to them to be asked their opinion and then to come up with solutions and make important decisions.

The longer kids are in an authoritarian institution that is imposing a curriculum on them, the more they get led away from themselves and from their confidence in themselves as individual learners. They start following the pattern of learning that they're expected to follow. John Gatto refers to this process as "dumbing down," and it really is a dumbing down process because kids who decide they want to learn something can learn at ten times the rate that kids learn in a regular public school classroom. It's really explosive.

For example, a student came to my old school in Vermont, Shaker Mountain, when he was around 10 years old, whom some people thought might be a little retarded. They weren't sure—he wasn't doing anything in school.

I tested him and his vocabulary was about normal for his age. In the first six months that he was at Shaker Mountain he didn't have much to say in the meetings but he was always in and around them, usually standing behind someone, but clearly paying attention, wanting to understand everything that was being said. Then six months later I gave him a routine vocabulary test and discovered that he'd gone up six grade levels in vocabulary in six months. I guess that would be probably 12 times the standard rate of learning. One part of this leap was certainly that he needed to understand everything that was being said in the meetings.

It is hard to fight against the inertia of our huge education system, this multi-billion, maybe trillion, dollar system that wants to maintain its own shape. You have to, at least initially, go outside of the conventional education system in some way. Which is why I think one of the greatest impacts on the system is coming from home education, where people have decided to check off "none of the above" and take the responsibility themselves for their children's education. This is also true, of course, of democratic schools and other various alternatives. All of these tend to come from outside the system.

I think of this analogy: the public school, or the educational bureaucracy, is like a giant balloon. If you have some innovation that starts at some point on the surface and starts pushing in and changing the shape of the balloon, you could probably push the innovation all the way through, even to touch the other side, but as soon as that innovation stops or that innovator goes away and the pressure comes off, the balloon goes back to its original shape. Just like any organism it gets used to being in a certain shape. That's what the education system does and that's why it's so difficult, if not impossible, to change that system from within. Anyway, the issue with kids is even more basic than that: it's an issue of human rights and children's rights. The fact is, kids have the right to be treated as adults would like to be treated: as human beings.

It is important to look at this in terms of children's rights. All people should have a basic right to have control over their own lives and their own education—up to the point at which their actions affect somebody else. When you look at it this way, you can't be exclusively concerned with how effective this particular approach is, whether it stacks up against one in which kids are pushed around and forced to learn certain things.

Someone recently sent me an email saying that he had polled about 50 people and asked them how they would feel if they were told that they had to go, starting that day and from then on, to a particular building and a particular room in that building and a particular seat in that room every day. This would be something they would have to do five or six hours a day for the next ten years. Of course, the reaction was that they would immediately call a lawyer or the ACLU. There could be no basis for such incarceration!

But of course this is exactly what we do when we start putting kids into compulsory school. And I do think that to a great extent it does come down to rights. For example, if you feel like working on your stamp collection, and that's how you'd like to spend your time, who is to say that you should really be spending your time joining a book club? It's just none of anybody's business.

Chapter Two
The Power of Democracy

Every school that says it is democratic has a different kind of meeting. One of the keys is to define, when you start—or even before you start—what decisions the meeting is going to have the power to make. It's very important not to imply that the meeting can decide anything and then have that not be the case. That can destroy the whole process.

It is possible to have a democratic meeting even when it has a very limited sphere of decision-making power, as long as it's clear what power it has and that power is never thwarted, co-opted, or counteracted.

People ask, "How can we do a meeting in a single classroom or in the family?" Well, you start out by saying to the kids involved, "These are the areas in which we can't empower you and these are the areas in which we can," and then be consistent—stick to what you've said. If you do that, then holding democratic meetings can be useful in almost any situation.

For example, for many years now I've been volunteering at the local Boys and Girls Club teaching table tennis. I'm only there two days a week for a couple of hours each day, but the club is open six days a week. I had taught the older kids for many years, 13-year-olds and older, and they would respond somewhat and then they would lose interest, and so I didn't come in all that often—I came when I had time. I never had a schedule for the first eight years I was there. When I started teaching the younger kids, there was so much interest that I had to commit myself to a real schedule for the first time.

Eventually I realized that the way to keep things properly organized would be to let decisions be made about the rules that we'd operate under for the table tennis club at a democratic meeting. The plan was that some of the kids could be elected as leaders or supervisors by the meeting.

This would seem to be a very limited area: we're talking about a table tennis club at a Boys and Girls Club that basically runs as an authoritarian organization in which there are staff who have the power to decide whatever they want. And yet, this became a powerful program because of democracy, and continues to be so.

As the kids have realized that every single one of their decisions has been implemented, without exception, the meetings have become increasingly complex and have gone into more and more serious philosophical questions. The kids have total faith in the meeting, even though these are all kids who go to regular public school classrooms. Many of these kids are low income, many are from minorities, but there's a pretty good mix of kids from all different backgrounds: some upper income kids, some white kids, a number of Hispanic kids, some black kids, and a few from other backgrounds, too.

The group has created a challenge ladder with 30 or 40 kids on it. A couple of controversies have swirled around the boy who was one of the higher players on the ladder. One situation happened when he let his cousin beat him and then he beat his cousin to bring his cousin up on the ladder. This was discussed at a meeting and I'll never forget this meeting because I've never been in another one like it.

We started out discussing the ethics of whether somebody should be allowed to do this, to organize to let someone beat him or her, and then beat the person back. We met in a separate room to start with, but we had to vacate the room halfway through the meeting and were forced to go out to the main room with all kinds of noise and chaos around us. The kids put seats in a circle and even though they had to yell to be heard, they would not leave the meeting until a decision had been made.

It was decided to make a rule against this activity, but that in this case there would be no consequence for the boy who did it because there had been no rule about it. From then on, if you broke this rule and you let someone beat you on purpose, you would go to the bottom of the ladder. This is an example of how seriously kids can take these kinds of decisions and the kind of process that is involved.

I was having a discussion with one of the Boys and Girls Club staff recently about the kids that we're working with. He had noticed really profound changes in some of these kids who had been pretty much out of control before they got involved with the table tennis club. I'm thinking of a few kids in particular who came to realize that in this situation the peers were the authority figures and that they had to listen to them and change their behavior.

In fact, a couple of these very difficult kids have been thriving. They've even been elected to positions like assistant supervisor or supervisor for the table tennis club. It's interesting that I didn't even know that one of those kids had previously been a problem kid, which is fine. That's the way I prefer it. I had high expectations for him, as I have for most kids. He's become responsible and attentive in the meetings.

One kid in particular, one of these two problem kids, was elected assistant supervisor even though people knew all along that he had various problems. He was cheating, they said, and taunting people and putting them down.

One day different kids made a bunch of complaints about him. At the next meeting he was put on the agenda to be talked about, but the kids did not vote him out as assistant supervisor. The meeting was more to give him feedback to let him know that he couldn't behave like that if he wanted to keep his position. The other kids knew he really loved it. To me this was a wonderful example of how to treat kids in a way that's effective and in a way that they can hear.

Even in this limited situation at the Boys and Girls Club, the kids have come to realize that they really do make all of the decisions to do with the table tennis club. They have never been vetoed by the staff. If something is not in the realm of what the kids can make decisions about, the adults are right up front about it. That's the key to having any effective meeting.

The problem with many meeting processes at different schools is that the powers-that-be pretend that the students have a broader area of decision making than they actually do. When the kids come to realize that they don't have as much power as they thought they had, or when something is countermanded or something doesn't happen that they've decided upon, the meeting process can be damaged.

In dealing with children who have difficult behavior problems, democratic schools need to use the democratic meeting. Other schools try to police those problems by guessing what rules they will need to keep everybody under some kind of control, a model that has limitations: sometimes they just don't guess right because they don't have everybody's input.

One of the things significantly different about democratic schools is that instead of having one authority figure you have the authority of everybody—all the kids and all the adults—making the decisions. This has a powerful impact on students, particularly ones who have had problems. Sometimes all of their energy has been going into fighting authority figures and so they really almost can't hear what the authority figures are saying to them. They certainly don't want to take it in or accept it because it's coming from the "enemy." But when it comes from peers, they can hear it.

People worry that kids' meetings will be boring because they've seen so many boring adult meetings. Any meeting can be boring if the meeting isn't relevant to the people listening. When I went to the Home Education Festival in England a few years back and was first demonstrating the democratic decision-making process, there were several hundred adults and about ten kids. When they found that we were going to discuss topics of interest to them, the kids came pouring in.

Later, when we had subsequent meetings about issues the kids were concerned about, the ratio was completely reversed and there were several hundred kids and just a smattering of adults at the meeting. This indicated to me absolutely that young people are not at all adverse to having this power or to spending time talking about difficult issues if they are truly empowered and if the topics are interesting and relevant to them.

Unfortunately, kids from public school, once they get to a certain age, don't seem to be able to work very well in a democratic community. Kids who have been disempowered by the public school system and have had a sense of loss of identity, sometimes need to be rebellious just to remind themselves of who they are. Conversely, though, most kids who have been in a democratic school for some period of time, if for some reason they need to be in any kind of authoritarian situation, can handle it just fine.

This is because when kids are constantly having to make decisions, they begin to know who they are, and to know how they feel about almost everything. When these kids go into an authoritarian situation, particularly if it's for a limited period of time, they do not feel threatened about losing their identity; they see the situation, instead, as a game that has to be played in a certain way. They're not worried about losing themselves in that process. I've had kids who came back from being in public school who said to me, "Wow, it's so easy. All you have to do is what they tell you to do."

Sometimes it was almost embarrassing because we had kids who would not only go on and do well in public school but would also go on to do well in the Army. I thought, "What are we doing? Training kids for authoritarian systems?" But these kids knew who they were, weren't concerned about losing their ultimate identity, and could use authoritarian systems for their own purposes.

There is no doubt that a rebellious kid is really just trying not to lose his or her own identity. That's one reason why the right teacher, who can recognize that, can get somewhere with that kind of kid. If a kid like that goes into an alternative school, especially when he is still young, he'll almost immediately have a total change in behavior. In a certain sense, what he was doing was a kind of civil disobedience in the context of the authoritarian system or the school he was in—an unconscious civil disobedience.

On the other hand, if this situation goes on long enough, then damage really is done to the person and it takes a long time to repair if she does go into an alternative school. At a certain point, it can be too late to repair the damage entirely and you may need more of a Band-Aid approach rather than a more thorough one. This is one reason why at my school we didn't take kids over 13 years old, unless they'd already had some experience in alternative education. And it's why Summerhill School, in England, for example, doesn't take kids over 11 or 12.

Once in the 1960s when I was working at Lewis-Wadhams School, I brought a couple of kids from Yellow Springs who were interested in the school; they spent some time at the school and were interviewed by the principal, Herb Snitzer. One brother was 16 and the other was 12 or 13. Herb was willing to consider the 12 or 13 year old but for the 16 year old he suggested that he just go to college, rather than try to get into a situation that would open up a lot of stuff that might take him many years to resolve. The boy went ahead and did that.

The longer you've experienced disempowerment and the abuse of an authoritarian system, the longer you've been having your own personality scraped away from you, your own identity taken away, the longer it's going to take to recover. Kids start out feeling they should be empowered and listened too. But, over a period of time, they can lose that.

Chapter Three
Democratic Community

A democratic community is a group of people who are empowered to make decisions about their community, hopefully a group of people that knows how to listen to each other. It can be made up of many different ages or different backgrounds. It can even be on the Internet or it can be an intentional community. And it can be a school.

There are some schools that don't technically make decisions democratically but where everyone really listens to everyone else and respects what others have to say whether they're adults or kids. Specifically, I'm thinking of the Stork Family School, in the Ukraine, which hosted the International Democratic Education Conference (IDEC) in 1998.

At the Stork Family School, kids and adults are mutually respected, and they were legitimately a host of the IDEC for that reason. They know there is something democratic missing in their process and it's something that they wanted to understand and learn more about.

But the mutual respect shown by community members means that they do things together without the adults being the boss. I've seen kids from the Stork School working late into the night with adults at conferences, writing songs and skits to be performed the next day, and doing it with complete equality.

What makes democratic communities dynamic is that a much higher degree of authority is involved in the decisions that are made. If instead of having one respected person making administrative decisions, you multiply that by all the other people in the community who are able to participate democratically, then there is much more authority behind the decisions. This is why democratic schools are able to be so self-disciplined, because so many people are invested in the outcomes of community decisions.

A democratic community doesn't have to be large. When I was home schooling my niece, Jenifer, we had family meetings to make decisions. Sometimes my sister was there. Sometimes my mother was there.

The key responsibility of students in a democratic school is that they have to be prepared to be fully-functioning members of their community. When they decide to join the community, they have to be willing not only to consider what their own needs are, but the needs of the community as well. Maybe they won't understand that immediately, but after some period of time if they don't seem capable of understanding that, then perhaps they shouldn't be part of that community.

Probably the most important marker of how well a community works is the quality of student leadership. Obviously, students will outnumber staff. If you have students who have been around for a long time and have seen the results of sweeping things under the rug, and they understand that it's important to confront things, then you will have a community that can function well.

If too many students within the community do not trust the democratic process, or if they're afraid to confront each other—because as a subgroup they want to support each other—then the democratic system tends to break down. Belief in democracy can be a delicate thing.

Peer pressure and conformity can happen anywhere, and all of this ebbs and flows, but generally speaking peer pressure is less likely to happen in a democratic school. Hopefully you've got enough people in the community who are not going to be affected by other people having a strong opinion about something. In my experience, there are always kids who are willing to express an opinion about things they disagree with, even if they are a minority of one!

But in some situations, there is pressure against people doing that. This is one reason why I tend to distrust consensus-type decision making: it can make people feel like they don't want to rock the boat, they don't want to be the one that blocks a decision, and so this might prevent them from giving an opinion that would totally change the decision.

In democratic schools you learn how to communicate with a variety of people, and to respect them too. It works well if you have an interesting variety of people in the community. There will be a carryover to anything that you do in life if you're able to communicate with people who are from different or unusual backgrounds; this carryover can be a direct result of growing up in and having been a part of a democratic community.

Democratic schools are using their meetings to teach communication skills. The point of doing it in a meeting structure is that you must stop and let the other person say what it is she wants to say without interrupting her. That changes the nature of the relationship of the two people, particularly so with adults who can dominate with the loudness of their voice or by interrupting.

As I said earlier, the key marker of the effectiveness of an alternative school has to do with student leadership. And this to me is a reason not to take a whole lot of older kids into a new alternative school. All schools eventually establish their own culture. If that culture is based on bringing in a lot of new kids who haven't had experience with democratic processes—disempowered kids who are going to carry in with them difficult previous experiences with authoritarian schools—you may establish a culture which in the end defeats the purpose of the school.

If you take younger kids, younger kids are closer to their feeling of their own authority, their own rights. That is a stronger thing to build a school on. Later, if you want to take older kids, you can do it occasionally, if you feel it might be effective for a particular kid. Often, though, you're doing a disservice when you take an older kid into a process that's thoroughgoing and could take years and years to work through. If you take a new kid of 16 or 17, maybe he won't actually be ready to move on until he's 25. But you're not going to have him until he's 25, so maybe you shouldn't take him into the school.

Staff have a tricky role at democratic schools, where the kids are really in charge. Often, each staff member has to work his or her role out individually. Adults have certainly had experiences that could be useful for the kids to know about. It is important for adults to communicate to the students what kinds of structures they have made for themselves in their own lives, what kinds of skills they have developed, what kinds of experiences they have had, so that the students can decide if these are things they want to find out more about. Adults should demonstrate, by the way they interact in the community, effective ways to deal with problems, solve problems, deal with crises, and deal with other people in a fair way.

It is important for kids to be able to have adults in the community with whom they can interact comfortably, adults from a variety of backgrounds, for the same reason I mentioned earlier: kids are going to need to interact with a variety of people later in life. The most important role for adults is to help kids get better at answering their own questions and meeting their own needs. The more kids can do this, the better. The less kids wind up feeling dependent on adults and what they know, the better.

The problem that you have, of course, in establishing a school, is finding adults who are able to fulfill that role, when most of them have not actually experienced democratic or alternative education when they were kids. That makes staffing a kind of a hit-or-miss thing.

One of the most important keys to teacher-student relations is that students should not be forced to go to any one teacher's classes. If the kids don't have to go to class, the teacher will eventually figure out what to do or what to offer that will be effective, and what he or she is doing that may be ineffective or counterproductive.

The parents' role can vary a lot according to how a school is set up. If a school is a parent's cooperative, they have a big role. For most democratic schools it's important that the parents, as much as possible, allow students and staff to make the decisions about the school. Parents should not be barred from going to the school and interacting as long as they do it reasonably. Of course the community can always decide if it feels a parent is being unreasonable.

It's very sad if the kid winds up being pulled out because the parent has been disruptive. And that does happen. One of the reasons is that parents sometimes live vicariously through their kids and try to get the freedom that they never had through involvement with a democratic or alternative school. At Shaker Mountain we set up a parents' group. They had control of their own parents' meetings. They could decide on projects that they wanted to do. But the parents did not have control of the school at all and we had no assembly, as Sudbury Valley School, in Sudbury, Massachusetts, has, with a lot of parents and teachers and students making overall policy decisions. At Shaker Mountain our trustees made those sorts of decisions; but the trustees, with students in the majority, usually referred important decisions back to the school meeting.

The kids at Summerhill do not get to make overall policy decisions or decide issues like the hiring and firing of staff. Some people think that this shows that Summerhill doesn't have a complete democracy. In many other schools, kids do have the ability to hire staff or have input into it in varying degrees. At Summerhill, founder A. S. Neill's idea was that there should be a basic environment and a routine that can be counted on, and that having this basic routine that kids can count on gives them more freedom. I've never bought this completely, but it's an interesting idea.

Within Waldorf schools, which follow the educational system designed by Rudolph Steiner, there is no democracy and not much of what I would call freedom. Students must go to classes and must do things in a certain way. The schools have a spiritual framework that creates certain restrictions in the way they do things. For example, according to their theories, little kids should only use colors in their art in a certain way; they can't use the color black. And they have to participate in a lot of the various activities. According to Steiner, this process in the end leads to a person who has more freedom. But if you haven't spent your life making decisions, where do you get the experience and the ability to start making them when you grow up?

In the same way, if a student spends 12 years in an authoritarian situation in a public school, where she is not encouraged to give her opinions, where she's assigned things to do, and where she has few day-to-day decisions to make, and then all of a sudden she is expected to make important decisions when she's 18, how is she going to do it? The logic is flawed.

Of course, schools can go to extremes in the opposite way, too. I visited a school called Summerlane many years ago, where the director seemed to me to be using the book *Summerhill* as if it were the Bible. If it was in *Summerhill*, then it was the rule, the law, the way that it had to be. This director was a Christian minister, so I think he was in the habit of following the dictates of a book, without question. Neill had to publicly dissociate himself from Summerlane when he heard wild stories about sex and drugs at the school. It was one of the first free schools to open in America and one of the first to close.

Neill, in *Summerhill*, introduced the concept, "freedom, not license." It's a good concept. The difference between freedom and license is to be found in the world of social interaction. You have the freedom to do certain things up to the point at which you're interfering with somebody else's freedom, and then some kind of negotiation needs to take place on an individual basis or in a democratic meeting. If you do something you want to do, but end up trampling over somebody else's ability to do what he wanted to do, that's license, not freedom. Playing music loudly in the middle of the night because you're staying up late and like the sound of it would be considered license if you end up keeping other people awake. On the other hand, if everyone else is on vacation and you're the only one there, it's freedom, not license!

Unfortunately, no particular action can be described as freedom or license in all cases. You have to look at the particular circumstance to make a judgment. Maybe the other person's perception isn't fair either! For example, what happens if somebody wants to go to sleep an hour before everyone else does? Do they have the right to tell everyone else that they have to be quiet if the rule for bedtime is for an hour later? The answer is not always clear. Each situation needs to be evaluated separately. If one boy arbitrarily and without negotiation decides he wants to go to sleep early and then he tells everyone else they have to be quiet or he'll get mad at them for not being quiet, this may be example of license. But what happens if that boy is really sick? Then the other people might decide they need to be quiet around that area. The decision needs to be made by the community.

Another circumstance might be if the boy had brought it up beforehand in the meeting. The meeting could decide this boy really needs to go to sleep early, he's not feeling well, or he has to get up early in the morning for some reason. For this one night the meeting could pass that this building has to be quiet after a certain hour—then it becomes a freedom again. So it's a totally fluid thing that's based on negotiation.

I suppose you could define freedom as a state of homeostasis, a state of balance within yourself and in a community. License creates imbalance.

Chapter Four
How to Run a Meeting

It's fine to have a large democratic school if you have good communications and a good way to get everybody involved in the meetings. You must have a comfortable room that's big enough to contain everybody. That is the limiting factor in a school. It has to be the same place where you can have your meetings every time and it has to be big enough so that everybody can come if they want to. Otherwise, the physical plant itself is limiting democracy.

When I went to the Home Education Festival in England, 900 people were there. When we held our meetings, eventually several hundred kids were able to come into the tent very comfortably to participate in the meeting.

At Shaker Mountain we never had a limit on who could speak or for how long. I used to keep track, though, and I found that generally speaking at our school the kids spoke about 60 percent of the time and the staff about 40 percent. That varied a lot according to the issues. As time went on, the kids were able to hold their own, and I don't know if that situation would have been improved in any way if the staff had bitten their tongues and stopped themselves from speaking.

Everybody who had an opinion was able to express it. It was up to the chairperson, however, if he or she felt someone had been talking too much to point that out to the person, or simply to call on more people to get a more balanced discussion going.

Some people worry that adults have more natural authority, so that kids will just blindly listen and follow them. That did not happen when I was at Shaker Mountain. A new kid might be influenced that way, but in general the students in the school would look at everything independently and would not be very influenced by what an adult had to say. On the other hand, some adults were respected because they had a good track record and people had found the things they said useful and believable.

An important stage that students would get to in the school was when they were able to criticize their friends in a meeting, if they felt a friend had done something that was not the right thing. This is an important point of maturity for anybody to get to, to be able to do this.

When the meeting was functioning well, people had no qualms about doing that and they knew they would still be friends with that person after the meeting. This is something that is not easy to achieve in a new democracy. When that happens, that's when you know that your democracy is working well.

At some schools—Summerhill is one of them—the Director and the staff have the power to make certain decisions that involve health and safety. At Shaker Mountain we found that our community was so sensible that whatever situation was brought up, the students would make good decisions about it. If anything, they almost tended to go beyond what we thought was possible.

For example, when it came to the question of drug rules, the kids understood that one of the most important things to the school was its public persona, its reputation. They knew this was directly related to how successful we'd be in fundraising, in getting support, and as they all knew, the school was not in any way supported by tuition. Fundraising was a crucial part of the school. Therefore, they felt it was imperative that the school not have the reputation of being full of druggies. They eventually passed a rule, which I have never heard of as being part of any other school, in which they said that even day school students had a 24-hour responsibility to the school as long as they wanted to be part of the school community.

This meant that if a day student did something that reflected badly on the school, even when they were on their own time, this could be brought up at a school meeting. I don't think any adult would have even considered such a rule, but this was something that came primarily from the students because they felt it was so important.

Problems with drugs and sexual issues were sometimes brought up in the meetings. If something was brought up and people thought it would be difficult for the parties involved to talk about it in a meeting, they could propose that we establish a small group of volunteers who wanted to work with the person or persons involved in that issue. The people involved had a right to reject anybody who volunteered, so the group would be people who were acceptable to the parties involved. Then, if necessary, the small group would come up with proposals to make to the meeting. This is how we dealt with things that we needed to go into in more depth than we could in the meeting itself. This could be for anything, but was usually employed when an individual student didn't feel like they could talk to the whole meeting about something.

Generally speaking, at Shaker Mountain, we were not allowed to have a meeting business about someone who was not actually there. The person had to at least be informed that there was going to be a meeting about them. However, if students were informed that the meeting was going to be about them, and they still did not come, then the meeting could make whatever decision it wanted to.

Almost no issue was too sensitive to talk about at our meetings; we talked about anything people wanted to bring up. Even things that would not ordinarily be brought to a school meeting, but to a board of trustees, were brought up, such as whether or not to buy a certain building. That was something we had a meeting about that was kind of a combination of the school meeting and the board of trustees. At Shaker Mountain five of the ten trustees were students in the school. This was something that was recommended to us originally by Harvey Scribner, then the Commissioner of Education in Vermont. So half of our trustees through all the years were students in the school.

Early on at Shaker Mountain it was passed that a meeting could not be held unless somebody was willing to take the logbook. It could be anybody, but somebody had to take the responsibility of recording what was discussed and what decisions were made in our blank, bound volume. To read these logbooks now is very interesting because whoever was taking the log would write his or her own editorial comments and draw funny pictures; students were allowed to do that as long as they got the basic information down about what was being discussed and what was proposed, what passed and didn't pass.

It is crucial to have a meeting record so that when people at a school want to look back and see what decisions have been made they can do so. Kids would often look back at the logbook to see, for example, whether somebody had a warning or a strong warning. It's interesting that at Shaker Mountain warnings were often debated very seriously. If you got a warning it would mean that if you did it again you could still get a strong warning, but if you got a strong warning and you violated that subsequently, then the meeting would have no choice but to take some kind of action against you in relationship to that violation of the school rules. There'd be a lot of discussion about whether somebody should get a warning or a strong warning and people would often look it up in the logbook to see what happened.

In a democratic meeting the chairperson has a crucial role. He or she really needs to know how to listen, and needs the reflexes of an athlete to do it right because there should be no time between one person finishing speaking and the next person being called on. The chairperson should also be aware of the order in which people have requested to speak. There are various ways of doing this; some people make a speaker's list. But I think it's better if the chairperson has more leeway; for example, they should be able to pick somebody who hasn't had anything to say yet rather than let the same few people who have been speaking keep on going back and forth. They need to be aware of how to keep the flow going and how to stay on topic, and should stop people immediately if they go off topic. At our school, where we had as many as 25 things on the agenda at a time, it was imperative to stay on topic. The chairperson needs to be able to stop somebody immediately and say, "Okay, this is not the subject we're talking about, but if you want we can add it to the agenda." It will sometimes happen just that way.

Because we had so many meetings and in so many different circumstances—on trips, at the boarding part of the school, and so on—people felt it was necessary for everyone to know how to chair a meeting. So when some new student would come in, she'd almost immediately be put to the test and she would get feedback and help on how to be a central part of this process. The majority of the students in the school eventually learned how to run a meeting well. Usually the students ran the meetings, and they could run them better than the staff.

Our younger students were some of the best chairpersons. They were usually the fairest and the quickest, and knew if something was going off topic. The interesting thing is that even at the Boys and Girls Club, one of the very youngest students is the most aware of sticking to the subject and making proper decisions.

Some schools run their meetings with the agenda decided in advance, others make it up right there. I believe you should have a combination; in other words, if people have something that they need discussed to be put on the agenda, that should be put on in advance and people should know about it. On the other hand I don't think it's right for people to have to wait too long to have something that they want to talk about come up. Some say you can't add to the agenda once it's set; I think people should be able to do that. If you have a community that has the will to make the best right decision about every subject that comes up, you can get through them fast enough.

The many schools that have been established on the Sudbury Valley model use a set system, the well-established Robert's Rules of Order. We did not really follow Robert's Rules of Order; we evolved our own system. This was largely influenced by our interaction and early communication with the Lewis-Wadhams School and later the Iroquois Confederacy, the Mohawk Tribe in particular.

One of the greatest influences on me was working at Lewis-Wadhams School, in the 60's, which was based on Summerhill in England. In Summerhill meetings, for example, they are allowed to have proposals against other proposals. Very often they'll have two or three proposals against each other. And sometimes they'd do "all against all" which means that if the majority of people are against all the proposals, then nothing passes. We used to do the same thing at Shaker Mountain School. If two proposals could legitimately be against each other, we could have them both on there. Or if they were not necessarily related to each other directly, so that they could stand alone, we could have several different proposals at a time and vote on them all at once, one at a time, rather than wait, as Robert's Rules says, for the next item to come up.

Personally, I think it's important that meetings be well structured and that they follow the structure consistently. Whatever structure is decided on, whatever has evolved, people need to be well versed in it. The meeting must be taken seriously. It should be quiet during the meeting so everybody can hear. One thing I found really useful when I had meetings with a very large group of students is a portable microphone so that even those with soft voices could be heard. I just heard about a fairly large charter school that is doing democratic process that has been using the portable microphone idea.

The way Summerhill controls noise is that the chairperson has the power to warn people and to fine them or kick them out of the meeting if they're being disruptive. I think that's up to each organization. At Shaker Mountain we never fined anyone because nobody had any money in our school, but people did get warnings and were asked to leave the meeting for a certain period of time if they had been disruptive. Then they could come back later if they chose. We do the same thing, by the way, in the table tennis meetings.

At Shaker Mountain we briefly tried having a separate meeting to discuss issues like bullying or stealing. Nobody liked it. Everybody wanted things to run through the regular meeting. So all of our decisions were either made that way or through a small group that would make recommendations to the meeting or try to resolve any disputes.

It's up to each organization or each school to decide how it wants to deal with these things. Some communities don't want to spend a lot of time dealing with petty disputes between people, or rather with disputes they consider to be petty. On the other hand, some people think it's important to understand what the community feels about whatever is going on, positive or negative.

Sometimes a child can benefit greatly from just sitting in a meeting and listening. One of the things that disturbs me about some big democratic schools is that such a small percentage of kids actually go to the meetings. They can say, "Yes, we're a democracy and people have the right to go to meetings." But it seems to me that if a school is so big that only a minority of the kids can get into the meetings, I think the school is too big.

Not that I believe in mandatory meetings, generally speaking. At Shaker Mountain meetings were not mandatory. However, if a particular issue came up about which it was felt that everyone in the school needed to be in on a decision, or to be aware of a particular situation, somebody could propose that the meeting become a "super meeting"; if the proposal passed, everybody who was in the school building needed to come to the meeting until it was voted that it was no longer a super meeting. Usually super meetings would not last too long and would be about some issue having to do with health or safety or something of that sort.

In our early years in Shaker Mountain, in our involvement with the Iroquois, we discovered an alternative to the usual "tyranny of the majority" type of democratic process. What we learned from them was that it was important to honor the minority. We would poll the minority after a vote and if they wished to say something more, they could express why it was that they voted in opposition. Then either they or anybody else in the school community could call for a revote. A revote would mean "with discussion" so it opened the subject up again and it was possible to make a new proposal and drop the original one or put a new proposal up against it. We found that this process was more thorough and that when we made a decision we were usually confident that we would not have to come back and revisit the subject. Only very, very rarely did we ever have to do that.

In my own experiences with communities using consensus instead of majority rule, I found it to be manipulative, and it sometimes prevented minority opinions from being expressed, whereas the minority opinion might become the majority opinion if people were able to say what was on their mind. I think ideally consensus can work well, but I've seen the process abused.

On the other hand, in a pure majority rule process, you often do not hear what the minority has in mind. People will say, "They had the chance during the discussion to speak their mind," but sometimes people just don't work like that. The vote gets taken, and all of a sudden it comes out that someone had a negative opinion but hadn't verbalized it.

With our Iroquois system, people who are unhappy with a vote get a chance to say what it is that is bothering them about it, or they can bring up another facet of the situation that hasn't been thought of. In this way we found that we often made decisions that nobody would have thought of in the first place. This is the great power of the meeting and it's this interactive process that is "more than the sum of its parts."

The Iroquois democratic process uses the best aspects of majority rule and of consensus. But in the end, at

Shaker Mountain, when the vote was finally taken, it would be okay if a decision were made by 25 votes to 23. If nobody in the 23 felt they needed to say why they voted the way they did, or if nobody felt they needed to call for a revote, then what it really meant was that those 23 were doing what the Quakers call "standing aside." They could live with the majority's decision and didn't feel the need to continue the discussion. But it also meant that the minority didn't have to pretend that they agreed with everybody. They could even eventually say, "I told you so," if whatever the majority had decided didn't work out well.

Our Iroquois process did take longer than the usual democratic meeting. For example, I'm always a little stunned when I go to the Summerhill meetings and see how quickly they make decisions. One of the things they tell me is that if they make a decision that is not the best one, they can then bring it up at a subsequent meeting and reverse it, and this does happen. It's not all that different, but our process I found was pretty thorough. We spent a lot of time in meetings, but it was my opinion that the meeting process was the most important educational process that happened at the school.

All kinds of real-life situations were brought into it and among other things, students had to develop a good vocabulary to understand what everyone was saying, and they had to develop good logical processes and look, for example, at the potential consequences of certain kinds of actions.

Chapter Five
Iroquois Democracy

Here is the story of how we heard about "Iroquois Democracy."

In 1968, a year when many new movements were born, I had just started Shaker Mountain in Burlington, Vermont, and we had four students. We all listened to a song recorded by Buffy St. Marie, called, "My Country, 'Tis of Thy People You're Dying." It was the story of Native Americans in the United States, but it was not the history of the Native Americans with which most of us were familiar. We wondered if it could really be true—that the white Europeans had so mistreated the natives of this continent.

Then one evening on the news we saw that the Mohawk Indians from a tribe in Upstate New York had blockaded a bridge that linked the part of their reservation that was in New York with the part that was in Canada because they were being charged taxes to go from one part of their reservation to another. We went over to the TV station in Plattsburg, NY and had them show us the segment they had just aired.

Not long after that we came in contact with a young man who was teaching in a public school near the reservation; one-third of the students at this school were Indians. (I've noticed that the Mohawks seem to be comfortable with being called either Native Americans or American Indians.) He invited us to come over to visit him and said he would try to introduce us to people who were "traditionalists," trying to keep the traditions of the Mohawks and Iroquois alive.

A group of us traveled over and stayed in sleeping bags on the floor of his apartment. He introduced us to a couple of key people he knew from his school who were involved in this movement. One of them was Ann Jock, the mother of several of the students in his public school. She was a clan mother in the tribe. Another was Tom Porter; we met with him in the Long House, where traditionalist Mohawks have met since before history was recorded on this continent. They have continued to hold their ceremonies and social dances there, dancing to music with lyrics so old that in some cases even they don't know the meaning of them.

This meeting with Tom Porter was a watershed moment for me because he introduced us to concepts I had never heard of before. He told us about the Iroquois Confederacy, which consisted of a number of tribes, of which the Mohawks were one. Other tribes had been invited to "take refuge under the Great Tree" if they were willing to follow the Great Law, which had been handed down to the Iroquois. The Great Law was a method by which people could live together in peace, not a racial concept but a spiritual one. In fact, the Iroquois had invited the French and the English to participate in this Great Law. They declined, and instead kept fighting wars with each other.

I subsequently discovered that Benjamin Franklin and Thomas Jefferson, when planning the fledgling affiliation of colonies that would ultimately become the United States, had carefully studied the way the Iroquois Confederacy was set up. In fact, Jefferson had such respect for Native Americans that he spent a lot of time traveling to a variety of tribes, documenting their languages meticulously. Unfortunately, years later when he was President and his documents were being shipped, robbers broke into one of the trunks that contained these papers, and seeing that they had no gold or booty in them, tossed them overboard. All that has been retained are a few of the papers that washed up on shore.

Tom Porter explained to us the way in which the Iroquois made decisions. They did not make decisions entirely by pure democracy—meaning majority rule. They would vote on proposals but then would ask those in the minority to explain why they voted the way they did. Then the whole group would continue to try to find a proposal that met everyone's need. The onus was on the minority to come up with a better proposal. Only when that was pursued as far as they could go would a final decision be made. It was this system that we adopted as the decision-making process in Shaker Mountain, and it stood us in good stead throughout the years.

That evening we were invited to go to the Indian Social Dance. We expected that we would be sitting in the audience and observing Native American dance done by people who had studied this and would demonstrate it. Little did we know that that was not at all the concept of Social Dance. When the dance started, we were all expected to participate and we did so. It was not all that difficult to simply follow what other people were doing. The sound of the music and the beat was infectious. In fact, as people danced the entire building would shake up and down. We had no option but to be involved with the beat and the movement!

Over the next couple of years we went back several times to Social Dances and got to meet people there and talk to them about our school. I sometimes suggested to them that perhaps they should think about creating their own school.

In 1971, I got an urgent phone school from Ann Jock at one o'clock in the morning. She told me that 70 Mohawk children had been kicked out of the public high school because they wanted to learn their own language and culture. At that time, Mohawk kids were actually punished if they spoke Mohawk in school because the teachers assumed that the kids were saying bad things about them behind their backs. Meanwhile, the language was dying and a whole generation of people no longer spoke the Mohawk language. Ann asked us if we could come to the reservation the next day, bring some of our students, bring slides, talk about our school and tell them how they could go about starting a school.

We made the two-hour trip the next day. We did a presentation in Ann's house, which was packed with parents and children. At one point we were asked whether they needed federal funds or state funds in order to start a school. We told them that they had the resources in their community to start the school and that it was not necessary to find government funds. A week later Ann Jock and her children (she eventually had 15 children) and several other children from the community started the Indian Way School in a small square building that they had constructed in their back yard. That building still stands and it has occurred to me that maybe it should be designated somehow with a plaque put on some national register because it was the beginning of the North American Indian Survival School Movement.

Over the next few years, and throughout the history of our school, we continued to have regular exchanges with the Mohawks at Akwesasne, which is the Indian name for the area of Upstate New York, and with the Kahnewake, another Mohawk tribe just outside of Montreal. They would come and visit us at our school in Vermont, and we would bring groups of kids from our school and visit them. A year after the first Indian Way School was started, a second one was started over the border in Kahnewake, known in Canada as Caughnawaga.

The school in New York never had any state funding and operated however they could on local funds. Ann had some problems because the traditionalist chiefs felt she had not contacted them first before she started this school and did not give her full support, and she had to struggle with that.

The Indian Way School near Montreal had more tribal support, but after operating for a year or so, they felt they wanted to try to get some funds to support it. A group of them traveled to Ottawa and went to the Bureau of Indian Affairs but were not taken very seriously. Coincidentally, at that same moment a group of Native Americans had taken over, by force, the Bureau of Indian Affairs in Washington, DC.

When they heard about this, the Indian Way School teachers said to the Canadian officials, "You know, we could have these guys here in four days." All of a sudden, they were listened to and they found a source of funding from the Quebec government that has continued to flow to them from that time on.

Because the people of the Indian Way School wanted their students to interact with kids from the dominant culture, but not from the public school mindset, they really liked having the exchanges with our school. This is why Ann Jock had originally chosen us as a model for what they wanted to do. For a long time the Indian Way School near Montreal was much better funded than we were, and they actually covered our costs so that we could travel to their "reserve" as they call it in Canada.

Not long after Ann Jock started the Indian Way School in New York, we raised some money for them to get off the ground even though we were having a hard time surviving ourselves. Meanwhile, at the Kahnewake

Reserve near Montreal, the other Indian Way School was thriving.

By this point René Lévesque, the Prime Minister of the Province of Quebec, had been elected. He was a proponent of Quebec separatism. He decided that all immigrants had to be educated in French in Quebec. He then decided that all Native Americans were immigrants. Well, even the non-traditionalist Mohawks knew they weren't immigrants and mounted a protest. They pulled their students out of the local schools, but since they had the Indian Way School as a model, instead of just keeping them out of school, they set up mini schools of about 15 students each across the reservation, led by Indian Way School staff.

After doing this for about a week, the parents were so surprised to see the positive changes in their children that they announced that this was no longer a protest, this was permanent, and that they were setting up the Survival School. The Canadian government, always happy to do anything that would oppose René Lévesque, said that they would pay for it. They eventually built a two-million-dollar plant along the St. Lawrence River, along with rope courses, a gymnasium, and a cafeteria, taking perhaps a third of the students out of the public schools.

Subsequently, the public school system agreed to create a total immersion Mohawk language elementary school option. They hired Indian Way School staff, particularly Rita Phillips who had been a teacher there for a long time, to write the appropriate curriculum. This option continues to this day.

Sometimes people wonder what the use is of setting up a small alternative school and keeping it going. In fact, the Indian Way School still continues, along with the Survival School and the public immersion Mohawk schools. This story shows that a small alternative model can lead to a change in the whole community. In this case it helped preserve the Mohawk language and culture.

Back at Akwesasne, the original Indian Way School had run for about six or seven years, but eventually closed. Then, around 1979, there was a big confrontation between the traditionalists and the elected system on the reservation. The politics on the reservation is difficult to describe, but one of the splits is along the lines of the imposed elected system and the traditional system, each with their own chiefs.

Very often those from the elected system would go along with the projects that the state and Federal government would be proposing, such as building bridges and roads through the reservation. They would rubber stamp these decisions. The casinos and bingos generally had been created by the non-traditionalists on the Mohawk reservations. Many of the traditionalists have resisted taking any funds from gambling. They also are opposed to drinking and drugs.

During this particular confrontation, the state police were called in, by the elected system, to reinforce them in an attempt to arrest some of the traditionalists. The traditionalists brought a group together in one segment of the reservation and set up an encampment that was reinforced by armament. They stayed in that encampment for a year and a half and during that time they created the Akwesasne Freedom School.

Having had the previous model of the Indian Way School, they knew that this was the kind of thing they could create if they wanted to. The Akwesasne Freedom School continues to this day. Around 1985, it became a total immersion Mohawk language school that has remained an independent school, although it has received some funds, from the Canadian side, through the Akwesasne public school board.

One evening we drove over to the reservation to go to Social Dance only to find that there wasn't one planned that evening at Akwesasne because "all the musicians had gone to the Island."

We asked them, "What island?" and they said, "Stanley Island." All of the islands in the St. Lawrence River belong by treaty to the Mohawks, but the administration had been taken over by the American and Canadian governments. The Canadian government was supposedly administrating the funds for this particular island.

The Mohawks had rented it out to white people who were not supposed to change it but had built a nine-hole golf course and twelve cabins on the island. The Mohawks were receiving a total of six dollars a year rent for this island. They felt that they had been mistreated yet again, and decided to go and reclaim the island.

A group of Mohawks had gone out to the island on a flotilla of boats, landed, and put up a big sign saying, "This Island has been reclaimed by the Mohawk Indians." At that point, the regular residents fled the island.

This was the island where all of the musicians were. They said to me, "Well, they know you. Bunny Arquette has a speed boat, go see him and he'll take you over there."

I was traveling with four students, two boys and two girls, and quite shortly we found ourselves on Bunny Arquettes' speedboat, heading for Stanley Island. We were welcomed when we got there and were given a large tent.

Shortly after we arrived we discovered it was a dangerous situation. The Canadian government had been paying non-traditionalist Indians to get drunk and come

51

out by boat and try to dislodge the traditionalists from the island. The boats kept on coming out and were being pushed off and there had been some fighting, even gunfire.

As it got darker, we started doing the Indian Social Dance around a huge fire, singing as loud as we could to scare away any new boats that might be approaching the island. By two o'clock in the morning they figured we were safe, because the bars were closed. A bit later, after we'd gone back to our tent, the kids and I could see some lights on small boats circling the island. "They're here!" one of the Mohawks whispered into the tent.

First one of these boats, and then another, made their way in towards the shore, and our tent was the first one that they would come across when they landed. We were scared; I picked up a piece of wood and got ready for action. But then to our relief we discovered it was just one of the traditionalists, checking the island.

The next day Bunny Arquette brought us back to the mainland. Any time I mention this story to a Mohawk, they will often ask the same question: "Are you Mohawk?" We were undoubtedly the only non-Mohawks to be on Stanley Island.

Chapter Six
Learning to Learn

Freedom for kids is important but democracy is the key. Democratic schools can even have compulsory classes—if a meeting made the ironic decision that they wanted to have compulsory classes. And, in fact, at Shaker Mountain we did have one compulsory class and a couple of other things that were compulsory, but these were things that were decided on by the school meeting.

Two or three times a week we had what we called the Must Do Class. The idea behind this was that it seemed worthwhile for us to commit ourselves to all sitting in a class for a forty-minute period during which somebody, staff or student, would make a presentation to us, usually on some subject we didn't know anything about.

It was the one class that everyone was expected to go to and put up with. Every year we would bring up the question of having the Must Do Class and of course at any point anybody could vote against having it, but people seemed to feel it was worthwhile. And I've already talked about how certain meetings were compulsory, when the meeting voted there had to be a super meeting or they felt that it was important that everybody in the school share some particular information.

Shaker Mountain was different from some other schools in that we never encouraged our teachers to teach in any particular field. If they knew something and somebody wanted to know about it, they could offer that. But we also felt that it was useful for teachers to teach things they knew nothing about, because one of the most important things to learn is how to find the answers to questions and how to find the resources you need. Sharing this experience with a learning adult can be very, very useful.

Some schools think it is important to have teachers available and waiting for kids to ask them for classes, rather than offering any set lessons. To me this seems as if the teachers are saying "Well, we have the answers but we're not going to tell you unless you ask us!" I think the students should be able to feel that staff members will share anything that interests or excites them personally.

Along those same lines, what is the responsibility of a school to its students in terms of creating an environment, or even giving them specific information about things that are possible, that they may not have known about and wouldn't discover unless someone took the time and almost forced them to learn? What happens if you are a teacher in a school and you see a certain pattern in a kid and you think it would be useful to them to point out that pattern?

It's not a simple thing and that's why teaching even in a free school is more of an art than a science. You have to know when, by almost reading somebody's mind or knowing them well, they would want to know some certain information or get some particular feedback and when it would be intrusive or stifling. There is a "when."

Still, I believe that I, as an individual and as a friend of a particular child, should not be reluctant to give him information, unsolicited, if I think I know what kinds of things he is interested in doing. But I admit that this makes the responsibility of the educator more complex.

For example, to what extent do you prepare the environment in a certain way? I wonder, but do not know to what extent the students at different democratic schools are involved in preparing the basic environment and to what extent the staff have the exclusive power to prepare that environment. Should school meetings get to approve every change in the physical plant or in the building?

I don't know the answer to these questions. If you hire staff members in a school, especially since the students are involved in the hiring, then you should trust them to do the work that you've hired them to do, which is to help prepare the environment and then be useful to the students in achieving the things they want to achieve. That may even include telling them about things they may never have heard of before.

Many schools use the painful fact that the older kids know they will soon be entering the real world to get them into line academically. I think schools make a mistake when they do that. At The Free School in Albany, New York, which only goes to eighth grade, they try to become a little more structured and make sure they're covering things when the kids get ready to go on to public school.

When Herb Snitzer of Lewis-Wadhams School was asked whether their kids were prepared to enter public schools he said the best training for a bad experience is a good one. So, if kids have a situation in which they are confident in themselves as learners, they can deal with anything. And that's been my experience.

It is clear that specific factual information is not very important in the information age when people can quickly get whatever information they need. How much information you've memorized doesn't matter so much anymore. The kind of testing emphasized by the new mandated high-stakes tests and the whole accountability movement is not only not important, but counterproductive.

On the other hand, knowing how to find information when you need it is important. And that could be tested for. Instead of knowing if children have memorized a fact, maybe they could be tested on how quickly they could find an answer to something they don't know. That is something that could be measured.

It may be possible to structure tests for real accountability in education, tests for things like responsibility, interpersonal sensitivity, humanitarianism, creativity. With a fair amount of thought these things that we really value in alternative education could be measured, and the public schools could be measured for them too.

I do believe in the Deweyan concept of having to evaluate or review what experiences you have had. That is one of the ways you really reinforce what you learn. We tried to do that in various ways at Shaker Mountain. One of them was our weekly evaluations, in which people wrote down the things they did during the week and discussed them with their counselor. That was an important part of our process.

People worry that kids who are not forced to learn will become lazy kids. Personally, I don't believe in the idea of laziness. I think that human beings have a tendency to do the things they like to do and are interested in doing. If kids grow up in a situation where they can continually choose the things they're interested in doing, they will not be seen as lazy. Not only that, but when these kids get into various situations later, they will be better able to find things that they are interested in doing because they will be used to that. If you force kids to study things that they are not interested in, they may come to appear to be lazy.

Some kids are more self-motivated than other kids, but it is very often the result of the experiences they have had, what kind of school situation they've been in, what kind of parenting they've grown up with, what their learning environment was like. But I've seen kids who were supposedly lazy become very self-motivated when they got into a situation in which they could really pursue the things they were interested in.

There was a boy at Shaker Mountain who had been there when he was very young, at about five years old, and then later, after having lived out of state, he came back again at the age of twelve. Through the first few months of that year it didn't seem he was doing much of anything in the school and in the meetings. He was there, but he would close his eyes and go to sleep. But whenever he was called on, he would immediately say (because there was a rule that you can't sleep in the meetings), "I'm not sleeping, I'm just resting." So they had to make a special rule for him that you could not "appear" to be sleeping in the meeting.

After a period of time there was a general agreement that he should go to a different school the next year because he didn't seem to be getting much out of ours. We did test him at the end of the year and according to my tests, he had gone up an average of three grade levels. He had been in fifth grade and would be going into sixth grade but we recommended seventh grade on the basis of the tests. He did so well once he started in his public school that they put him in eighth grade.

So he really had gone up that far in an almost mysterious process. I don't think that it's necessarily something that we can control. It is freedom that is the key to unleashing this power that all kids seem to have.

In order to graduate from Shaker Mountain, because there was no set curriculum, one of the things that students had to do was demonstrate a certain academic proficiency. One of the ways to do that was to take and pass the GED, or high school equivalency test. There were inevitably certain subject areas that students had not been involved with during their time at the school.

As a general rule of thumb, the students would tell us what they were, we'd set them up with a study program, and they'd learn the equivalent of one full year's schoolwork, in that subject, in about three weeks. This would go for almost any subject area that they wanted to tackle.

This reminds me of another story. A student came into the school way behind according to standardized tests. He seemed to be doing okay in the school but we weren't sure how much he was catching up academically. When he got to be 16 or 17 years old he announced to the school community that he intended to graduate the next year. People were skeptical because they knew he would have to take and pass the GED test and he was far from being able to do that.

Over the summer, he was determined to learn everything he needed to learn in order to do that, and when he came in at the beginning of his final year he took and passed the GED test without any problem. He had taught himself everything he needed to know over the summer.

Even though he had passed his GED, people pointed out to him that there were other aspects of the graduation requirements that he needed to fulfill, mainly showing a certain degree of responsibility. So he did several things that year. He took responsibility as the clean up supervisor. He started his own little shop buying and selling collectible cards. And at the end he did graduate that year.

Immediately after graduating he went to work at a local department store that had just opened up. They put him in as a stock clerk and he did a little work there. At one point, when someone was having trouble clearing the cash register, he came out and showed them how to do it and got it straightened out. Within a short period of time they made him a floor supervisor at the age of 17. The way these sort of businesses work, it's hard to find anybody to take proper responsibility for things and do it with confidence. Among other things, he was responsible for all the suits that were being sold on that floor, even though I don't think he'd ever worn a suit in his life before he went to work there!

Chapter Seven
Shaker Mountain

After college I visited Lewis-Wadhams School and they invited me to work there for a term. I wound up getting paid a lot less for it than I would have working at my uncle's company but it was a turning point for me because I was definitely moving away from science and toward education at that point. This was in 1964. Lewis-Wadhams was in its second year. I was still an undergraduate, at Goddard College in Vermont.

Herb Snitzer had been in England doing a book of photographs of Summerhill called *Summerhill, A Loving World.* When he got back here he decided to start a school with his wife, Kate. A.S. Neill's daughter Zoë had come over and worked as a houseparent the first year and then gone back to England. She was not there when I arrived.

The school had been closely based on Summerhill, so I learned a lot of things about Summerhill from my experience with Lewis-Wadhams. They had a meeting bell and even the way the meetings ran was very much how Summerhill did things. Many of their little traditions came from Summerhill. Certainly my experience at Lewis-Wadhams was very important for me, in terms of my attitudes about democratic education and learning. The school ran successfully for fifteen years.

I had my disagreements with Herb and Kate—I wanted eventually to start a school that wouldn't just be for kids who could afford a school like that—but basically it was a terrific school. Even to this day there's an alumni organization on the Web and people look back very fondly on their experiences there. We sent two or three students to Lewis-Wadhams from Shaker Mountain.

Herb, while he was at Lewis-Wadhams, pretty much put his life as a photographer on hold although I clearly remember him making portfolios of the photographs of Summerhill that people would order. That's when I really learned about art photography, especially as I watched him making some individual pictures and putting his hands through the light, almost like a conductor or painter, so that certain areas would get more exposed than others when he was enlarging and making the prints. Obviously no two prints were alike. He was a student of Ansel Adams, one of the greatest photographers of the last one hundred years.

After I got my Master's Degree at Antioch I worked for a while at Elm Hill, the first group home for state foster children in Vermont, and helped it get off the ground. It was based on my Goddard college thesis and continues to this day as Maple Hill School. But I needed to go off and do something on my own. I wondered if it would be possible to do something with a similar philosophy to Summerhill in a public school so I got a job working with remedial reading students and underachievers at Champlain Valley Union High School in Hinesburg, Vermont.

I did that for a year and had very good results with the kids and ran the program like a free school within the school. Because I ran the program during their free periods, every kid was in there by choice. I wrote a little diary about it called, "I Was a Spy in the Public Schools." Over time I realized that in a public school it was more likely that the system would change you than that you would change the system.

The next year I was given a job as a teaching principal in the next town over, Starksboro, and my father helped me buy a house in the town. A year later, in 1968, I started Shaker Mountain.

We started small. At first we met in different spaces and traveled around in our car. That was the basic setup in the beginning. We had a Plymouth and we almost decided to call the school the Plymouth School. That was before we got the storefront building at 86 Pitkin Street, which I think was about six weeks into the year.

We had no boarding students until the third year. But we did have staff who lived at what would become the boarding part of the school, out at my place in Starksboro. That's about all we could provide because we didn't have much money.

Over the years we found an approach that really worked well. Of course the decision-making process evolved, but the concept that we pioneered and came up with, which was inspired by the Iroquois, held us in good stead all that time.

I ran the school for 17 years, until 1985, and it actually ran for a while longer. I had then gone to work temporarily to help the National Coalition of Alternative Community Schools, which needed a director. So I took a leave of absence and the school continued on to the next year organized by a couple of parents. But they pretty quickly made changes in the school and went through a lot of the money that we had built up. When I came back we tried to find other people who could direct the school and keep it going, but we were unable to do that.

There were good years and bad years at Shaker Mountain and it partly depended upon the quality of student leadership at the time. For us the meeting was the most educational aspect of our school. It certainly is the thing that we spent most of our time on and really specialized in.

The value of the meeting goes beyond education, obviously. It goes right to the empowerment of each student—and each staff member, for that matter — and to the respect for each individual, and to their rights as a member of the school community.

We had two long staff meetings every week, which was important in terms of communications within the school. The kids were allowed to be part of the staff meeting unless it was closed for specific business. We always found that the kids' input into the meeting was valuable because they knew a lot of the things that were going on that the staff didn't know.

We tried not to have meetings every day, but we did have a Monday morning and Friday morning meeting, each of which would have many items on the agenda. That's where all of the decisions that ran the school were made.

At Shaker Mountain you could call an emergency meeting any time you wanted to and the way you would do that was simply to ring a meeting bell, which was an old fire bell. You didn't have to get someone's permission. At Summerhill, for example, it used to be that you had to get permission from the chairperson to call a special meeting. I don't know if it's that way right now.

Our rule was if there were classes going on, people did not have to leave the classes to go to a meeting. Whoever went to the meeting, whoever was there, would make the decision for the school. Permanent decisions about the school could not be made unless they were at one of the regularly scheduled Monday or Friday meetings. Decisions that were made in the interim were reviewable by the regular meeting.

Somebody asked me once, "How did you stop people from ringing the bell when there wasn't a meeting?" I told them that we had made a special rule about it. If you rang the bell when there wasn't a meeting, there was an automatic meeting on you for ringing the bell when there wasn't a meeting!

At the start of our meetings whoever wanted to be chairperson would say so. The whole process took place very quickly. One of the reasons for that was that we had lots of meetings and there wasn't great prestige in running a meeting. It was hard work. People were aware of that, but they also wanted to elect a good chairperson so the meeting would go smoothly. So several people would usually say they wanted to be chairperson, there would be an immediate vote, and whoever got the most votes would simply start chairing the meeting.

If that person got tired at some point, they could give the chairpersonship to somebody else. Or if somebody thought the chairperson wasn't running the meeting well or that his or her attention was lagging, anybody could call for a new chairperson at which point there was a vote immediately, up or down. If the majority did not want to vote for a new chairperson, the chairperson simply continued.

The chairperson would go through the agenda while the log-taker kept track of all the items on the agenda. The chairperson's job was to keep people on task, on the subject, keep everything moving smoothly, call on people in order and bring items of business to the vote. If you had a specific question to ask somebody during a business, the person could answer that question—they didn't have to wait to be called on.

Sometimes the chairperson would ask another person to keep track of the hands to make sure she got the order right. Generally she would follow that order unless there was some important reason not to. For example, if the meeting was about a particular person, she might let that person respond more often.

Every morning there were class announcements. There was no set curriculum and we had few classes that were regularly scheduled, or if they were, it would usually just be for a week or two. Otherwise, there were just class announcements every day, and there was no pressure for anyone to go to any of those classes. Any activity whatsoever was called a class. So going to play racquetball was called a class, organizing a trip to the Bahamas was called a class. Eventually we had three vans available all the time, so the vans were constantly going off all around the city to different places or activities, and these trips were called classes too.

We designed our curriculum retroactively. At the end of the week we had evaluations in which we made a list of the things we had done that week and each student picked a counselor who was one of the staff who would go over any individual problems or questions and would help them do their evaluations. It occasionally happened that a kid didn't want a counselor, but not usually.

At the end of the year we made a list of all the different activities, around 350 a year, and the kids would check off all of the things that they had done and that would be used for transcripts. In fact, in some cases, if a student needed a transcript, we'd have them write their own.

I always used to be so surprised at how lucky we were to get good teachers in my school though we paid far less than any other local school paid their teachers. Over a period of time I came to realize several things. One is that it wasn't just luck. We had a system in which teachers received intensive feedback, in and out of the staff meetings. Often the new teachers who came in weren't very good teachers. Soon they were getting instant feedback because no students would go to their classes. They made changes and became good teachers or they would discover that they couldn't do it and leave.

Many teachers in the public school system never learn that lesson because they have a captive audience. I do think one of the key factors in the training and development of alternative school teachers is non-compulsory class attendance.

Another factor I mentioned earlier is that because we paid so little we almost never would get a teacher who was there because of the job or the money. They were there because they believed in what we were doing. This was the way they had to teach because they wanted to be in a situation that was empowering students.

A couple of times when we edged to the point where we were almost paying what somebody might get paid elsewhere—there were a couple of years when we were getting what was called CETA funds and salaries actually went up to something like $125 a week—we got a few teachers who were there for the job. We came to realize that they probably wouldn't have come were it not for the "decent" money.

Obviously the teaching of classes wasn't the only thing teachers needed to be able to do; they had to be able to get on with individual kids, as well, and with the other staff members. They also needed to be getting something out of the experience themselves.

At Shaker Mountain we used to have something called the Stop Rule. The Stop Rule was based on the idea that, for a lot of kids, when they got into some sort of a conflict it was because they hadn't clearly communicated to the other person how they were feeling. For example, sometimes kids would be wrestling and they'd be having fun. Then all of a sudden one of the kids didn't want to wrestle anymore, but the other kid didn't realize it. Then the first kid could say, "Stop," and that would communicate in one word all of the possibilities: I don't want to do this anymore, I'm being annoyed by it, I feel like I really want to fight about it, whatever.

If someone said the word "Stop," it would mean that the other person had to stop doing whatever it was he was doing. If a problem continued, it would be brought up in a meeting and people at the meeting would say,

"Did you use the Stop Rule? Did you say Stop?" That was always a key question. And the next key question would be, "And did they stop?" If you didn't stop when somebody said Stop, you would be breaking the Stop Rule, which was a serious transgression and put a lot of the moral force against you.

But then a bunch of other rules were made that involved abuse of the Stop Rule. For example, you were not allowed to use the Stop Rule if it was asking somebody to do something that was unreasonable. For example, I couldn't say to you, "Your breathing is annoying me. Stop breathing." That would be abusing the Stop Rule. There were some kids who would abuse the Stop Rule by initiating some kind of contact or fight and then saying, "Stop," so the person couldn't react back to it. That was considered abusing the Stop Rule. All these things got pretty complex but they got worked out.

We had a long trial period for anyone wanting to get into the school, and an admissions committee that would decide who was accepted. There was first a visiting week after which the admissions committee would decide if it had been successful. If it was then the prospective student would have a trial week.

We were able to extend either the visiting or the trial week. The basis on which it would get extended was if a person showed that he or she was not able to have the controls to show responsibility during that period of time. We knew that anybody who wanted to get into the school would perhaps try to put on a nice act for that first week or two and then other stuff would come out later. Our basic opinion was that if someone couldn't even put on that act for a week or two, he or she probably didn't have the basic control needed. So that was the rule of thumb we used.

A community needs to recognize when a particular individual ought not be part of that community. Perhaps she ought to leave for a period time or find a place that's more suitable to meet her needs. This is sometimes hard for schools to do and it has been the downfall of several schools where they just didn't have the mechanism to do this. Communities have kept working with people for too long, to the point where their whole structure gets torn apart.

This is one reason why the admissions committee would extend the trial period for so long. It was unusual for anybody to actually be turned down by the admissions committee. It was ordinarily more of an educational process.

If it seemed like the school really was the wrong place for them, sometimes the meeting would actually send kids back to the admissions committee for another trial period, to see if they could develop the controls to come back as full members of the community. It would be almost as if they were a new applicant to the school again and the admissions committee could decide that they were not accepted and they would have to go someplace else. This did not happen to a large number of kids.

I noticed an odd thing happening, that was amazing to me and that I could only see in the long sweep of time. Someone would get kicked out of the school, after the meeting had done a good job of bending over backwards to make sure the person got as much due process as he could and with people having tried to make a good transition for him to whatever other situation he was going to go to. Five or six years later that person would come back to the school wanting to be a staff member. Or at least come back and touch base with us and tell us what happened subsequently. Very rarely would he have any anger or bitterness towards the school. I think that process has to be done well, and we usually did do it well. It was almost as if the community had set a standard for them, and they came back to tell us that they had finally reached it.

Maybe at the heart of all this is the idea that once you get brought into a community, even if eventually the community has to reject you, in some way you will always be part of the community. You become part of the fabric.

Many of these kids, particularly with the boarding students, were kids who'd had very difficult life experiences before they came to us. They'd been abandoned, abused, and so on. This is something you see in many alternative schools, not just democratic schools.

It is remarkable to me that kids who had difficult backgrounds and became boarding students have lived their subsequent lives as if they had been in a privileged, nurturing environment, as if they had been in a nurturing family. They have not been self-destructive or depressed or anything like that. On the contrary, they have been successful in their lives. I think this is a clear indication that we did operate as a kind of nurturing family and those kids, generally speaking, were always thankful that they had been raised by Shaker Mountain.

We never thought of ourselves as being anything other than a school even though in some ways we functioned as sort of an intentional community. The same thing is true of The Free School in Albany, New York, and of Summerhill, and of a lot of other good schools.

Any group of people living or working together is a community. I would even go beyond the word community and say that in a lot of ways what we were like was a big family.

Chapter Eight
Connections Beyond School

People worry that alternative schools can be isolated communities. I do get concerned about schools which, for example, are not doing a lot of field trips, not going out into their communities a lot, and are pretty much staying in their building. In the end, of course, the kids are still going to be able to cope with whatever situation they have to deal with, if the basic process is good. But it is better if you have a school that is interfacing a lot with its community.

This is what we did at Shaker Mountain. We were right in the downtown of our city, so people couldn't really ask the question, "What happens when you're in the real world?" because students were continuously going off to do internship jobs or going to the library and other places in the area, and using them as resources. In addition to that, probably half the school was off in the community every day. We had three vehicles and they were being constantly used to go places and do things. I think that's a better situation, if it can be arranged according to the circumstances of the school.

Here is an example: one day a student named Danny came into school and was asking what he would need to do to get a pilot's license. So we went yelling around the school for anyone who was interested in "Danny's Pilot License Class" to get into the van. Then we tried to figure out where we ought to go. We decided to go to the local airport and ask them what someone would need to do to get a pilot's license.

At the airport they said that there was a program for that kind of training next door. So we went next door and talked to the manager of their flight-training program.

He explained to us what someone would need to learn, and told us trainees had to fly so many solo hours. Then one of the pilots came in and the manager said to him, "Why don't you show them the cockpit?"

So we went out with the pilot to look at this small plane that he'd just been flying in. The manager yelled out the door, "Why don't you take them for a spin?" So we wound up flying over our school—and this was probably within an hour of the time that Danny asked how he could get a pilot's license! This is the kind of thing that you would not have happening in an ordinary school. Anything was possible. The sky was not a limit!

At Shaker Mountain when we traveled in small groups we would have trip meetings. One thing that was different about that from our regular school meetings was that when we were on a trip it was understood that whoever organized the trip, usually a staff member, had the power to make decisions for the group, especially in urgent situations. We couldn't be stopping every five minutes to have a meeting to decide things.

It was expected that when there was time we would have meetings to resolve any particular situations that came up. That made the situation a little different, because the trip organizer did have that power. This would have to be formally acknowledged by the people who signed up to go on the trip. The kinds of things that usually were decided democratically had to do with what things we wanted to do and where we wanted to go in general, and also interpersonal things.

Once, on a trip meeting, we were having problems with a particular kid. I was usually careful only to bring students on trips who had already been in the school for a while, kids who had resolved a lot of their interpersonal problems. On this particular occasion, we brought a new kid who began to do his acting out process on the trip. One time on this trip we had to have a meeting while driving that lasted from Florida to Georgia. It must have been two or three hours that this meeting went on as we drove along in the van.

Another time someone brought up in a meeting, at the school, that they would like to have us go on a school trip off the continental United States. At Shaker Mountain we did a lot of traveling and we had already been almost every place you could go by van in North America. We had been to Florida, California, Mexico City, British Columbia, Vancouver, New Brunswick, Prince Edward Island, and Nova Scotia.

We batted this around for a while, a trip group was announced, and in the trip group we discussed some of the closest places we could get to, out of the USA. We looked at a map and realized that one of the closest countries off the continent would be the Bahamas.

Of course at that point, and throughout the history of the school, we had no budget for travel. If we'd had a small budget, we would probably have been limited as to where we could go on school trips. However, since we had no budget whatsoever, we could go anyplace we wanted to!

There was no limit because it was incumbent upon each trip group to come up with their own funding. And the students at Shaker Mountain developed many different ways of funding their trips. Sometimes they would do things in advance, having an auction or a special event of some sort. Sometimes they would get local sponsors. For this they would have a sponsor sheet, which would say, "I'm a student at Shaker Mountain School and I have a chance to go on a trip and would you be interested in getting involved in the process of sponsoring me?" We would sometimes raise quite a bit of money in a short period of time.

In this case we made a phone call to an 800 number for the Bahamas Tourist Bureau and asked them whether, if we came to the Bahamas, they would be able to find a place to put our sleeping bags down and places where we could speak about alternative education. They got back to us and said that the People to People Organization would be very interested in having us come, that they had places for us to speak, schools that were interested in having us visit, and that the Orange Hill Guest House had agreed to let us stay there, with our sleeping bags.

We called the airlines and said that the people of the Bahamas had invited us to come there, that they have places for us to sleep, places for us to speak, and schools to visit—all we need is transportation. The first couple of airlines turned us down but the third one we called, Bahamas Air, said they might be interested in helping us but that they only flew from Miami. Of course our school was in Vermont, 1500 miles away.

We had a trip meeting and made a decision about what to do. We voted to go for it. We decided to work our way down to Florida and hope that perhaps Bahamas Air would be able to make some kind of arrangement for us.

So we worked our way down the East coast, speaking at colleges and passing the hat, stopping at restaurants and cleaning parking lots in exchange for meals. And finally we made our way all the way down to Florida.

At one point, on the way down, we called the airline's public relations person and told him we were on the way to Florida. He now said he would be able to give us the tickets at half price. We told him to forget it. We couldn't afford that. These were low-income students. He told us to keep in touch.

We actually went past Miami into the Keys. We found a motel that had some rooms that they weren't going to be able to clean till the morning and the kids talked them into letting us put our sleeping bags down there. The students got good at doing those things. I think if you can do that, you can talk to anybody in life about anything.

Then we called the public relations person at the airline again and he said that he would donate all the kids' tickets but we had to get to the airport in Miami the next day. So we drove up to Miami and got on the plane. They flew us to the Bahamas.

We were met by the Lutheran church bus which took us to the Orange Hill Guest House, right on the ocean. Then they started taking us around the island to the various schools that we wanted to visit. They even had a banquet at one of them in our honor.

It was a great trip but in some ways quite a shocking experience for our students, and an interesting one, because they came from a state that was 99 percent white and they were now in a country that seemed to be almost the same percentage black. I remember a kid at one of the schools in the Bahamas asking one our students, "What do you do if they call you a honky?" And the Vermonters looked at each other blankly. We were there for five days, then we flew back to Miami and we worked our way back up to Vermont.

Chapter Nine
Alternative School History

People often ask: "How did the democratic school movement get started?" Well, I'm not a historian. The whole idea of democratic process is one that always seemed obvious and natural to me. For example, when I started my first recreation center, when I was at Goddard College, it ran as a democracy. This was before I had ever read *Summerhill* or heard of it. When I started Shaker Mountain, I don't think that I was aware that there was any kind of large movement of free schools. This was probably true of many of the other thousands of people who started little schools. Only gradually did we realize that there was some kind of movement and try to coalesce and organize it in some way.

I just was reading a statistic that in 1902, 95 percent of the births in the US were home births. If you go back another 50 or 75 years—to the mid-19th century, probably the large majority of kids were educated at home in one way or another.

Way back in 1762, Rousseau wrote in *Emile* that kids ought to be educated with freedom. In the 1830s, Bronson Alcott had a little school that was experiential in its orientation and respected the students' rights. At one point, though, he took in a black girl and a number of his students left. Pretty soon he had only about six kids. One of them was his daughter, Louisa May Alcott, who went on to write *Little Women*. The companion book *Little Men*, where her fictional character Jo ran a school out of her home, actually also had some influence on people in terms of starting alternative schools.

One of the pioneers in this approach was Francisco Ferrer who started the Modern School. He was an anarchist in Spain and he was doing work with kids in the early 1900s. He was shot in 1909 on the trumped-up charge of plotting to kill the king. His last words were, "Long live the Modern School." In his name they established the Modern School movement. At one point there were as many as 200 in Spain and many others were established around the world including one in New York City, which eventually moved to Stelton, New Jersey. They continue to have Modern School alumni reunions every year, even though some of the people there are very, very old.

The last Modern School, which closed in 1958, was run by Nellie Dick. She died in 1995 at 102 years old. The Ferrer schools were very specifically democratic. Other pioneers in alternative education around that time included John Dewey, Maria Montessori and Rudolf Steiner—but democracy wasn't a part of their approaches, though Dewey wrote a book called Democracy in Education. Dewey was more concerned with trying to prepare kids for democracy when they grew up.

I first heard of Dewey when I went to Goddard College in 1960. Dewey, of course, was the person who created the idea of progressive education. He was picking up on the fact that children are natural learners. Dewey's work goes back to before the beginning of the 20th century and many schools were inspired by his ideas. A few of these schools continue to this day and are generally called "progressive" schools.

A commonality shared by all the people who have approached this important reality of alternative education is that children are natural learners. The original definition of the word 'education' related to the concept of educing or drawing out of people the learning that is inherent in them. The public school system has the opposite assumption. They think of children as empty vessels that need to be filled up with facts or information, rather than as people who already have a natural curiosity and interest in learning.

One of the many schools in New York City that was inspired by the progressive movement is called City and Country. It was started before the First World War and continues to this day. It is still one of the better alternative schools in New York City. Other schools in New York, such as the Little Red Schoolhouse and the Bank Street School, were originally inspired by Dewey and his idea of progressive education. Dewey's basic idea was that kids learn best from direct experience, from taking some responsibility, and from working directly with their hands.

In many of the progressive schools the kids were on a first-name basis with their teachers and they did not have grades. As a result, in the 1930s, American colleges had a lot of kids applying to them without any grade history.

They wanted to figure out whether this system was a good one or not and how to judge the students. So they created something called the eight-year study, which stands today as one of the most definitive studies of a learner-centered approach, as opposed to a curriculum-driven one. The results of the study showed that students from progressive schools did better in college, and after college, than the kids from the traditional schools.

John Dewey was born in Burlington, Vermont and he eventually wound up teaching at the Columbia University Teachers College in New York City. One of his students was Royce Stanley Pitkin. Pitkin was from Marshfield, Vermont; he studied under Dewey and subsequently went back to Vermont.

In Barre, a small city near where Pitkin was born there was a struggling school called the Goddard Ladies Seminary. He decided to take it over and make it into a progressive college. He bought some land that was a former estate in Plainfield, Vermont. There was an old huge barn and the main house and several other big outbuildings. Late in life John Dewey came up to help Pitkin organize and conceive Goddard College, helping to create it as a progressive college.

When I went to Goddard College, in the early '60s, I became interested in education and studied under Pitkin. I took courses from Pitkin about John Dewey. In my final year at Goddard, my thesis was called "On Starting a School," which was becoming my firm intention. After I had spent a work term at Lewis-Wadham School in New York, I had made up my mind.

Eventually Pitkin, after he retired from Goddard College, came back to Burlington to speak at one of our graduations at Shaker Mountain School. His talk was on John Dewey and what Dewey was like. He said Dewey was highly critical of standardized testing, even back then.

He talked about something that had happened in Texas—if we wondered why he picked Texas rather than Vermont it was because he didn't want Vermonters to look stupid. He said in Texas they measure the weight of a hog by taking a board and putting it over a rock. On one side of the board they put a hog and on the other side they'd place a boulder, to balance the weight of the hog. Then they try to guess the weight of the boulder.

That was his criticism of standardized testing: he felt it worked just like that. He also told us that John Dewey was not an exciting speaker: he would fix his eyes up on some far point on the ceiling in front of him and just stay looking like that the whole time he was talking. It was not always easy to follow everything he had to say.

There was something significant about Pitkin coming to speak about Dewey at the Shaker Mountain graduation. It completed a circle for me, because my school was one block away from where John Dewey was born.

In the early 1960s the free school movement was definitely jump-started with the publication of the book *Summerhill*. Thousands of free schools were created within the next fifteen years, inspired by *Summerhill*. Most of them didn't stay open long. Eventually, because of the free school movement, many people decided to try to do something like that in the public schools. That led to the alternative school movement, which continued on into the '70s.

Summerhill was the first specifically democratic school and it is certainly now the oldest; it was established in 1921 by A.S. Neill. Neill was a Scottish teacher who had decided from his experience that he did not want to replicate the kind of education that he'd grown up with. In England he became a famous radical writer on education before he had any thought of starting a school. This was in the years leading up to the First World War.

At that time he was very much influenced by Homer Lane, an American who went to England to start a therapeutic community for troubled youth, called The Little Commonwealth. Homer Lane had already created similar democratic programs, within reformatories for boys, in the United States. Neill's school was directly inspired by The Little Commonwealth and Homer Lane.

Neill actually first started his school over in Germany. When he moved back to England a few years later his school got the name Summerhill. During the early years of the school he wrote many successful books about his experiences but never had any publishing success in the

United States until the compilation *Summerhill* came out in 1960.

Neill was 38 when he started Summerhill and he ran it for 52 years until he died at age 90. His friend John Aitkenhead did almost the same thing with Kilquhanity House School in Scotland, which was a sort of sister school to Summerhill. It ran on a similar system from the start of the Second World War. Quite recently, when John Aitkenhead was an old man, government inspectors demanded compulsory lessons and forced Kilquhanity to close.

I never got to talk to Neill and never corresponded with him. I met Ena Neill, his wife, in the '70s, after Neill's death, and she was clearly a tough, strong woman. Her teamwork with Neill had a lot to do with how well Summerhill was run and how it has been able to survive. Ena had always done a lot of the nuts and bolts work to keep the school going. After Neill's death Ena ran the school until the mid-'80s, when their daughter Zoë took over the school. Ena died in 1997.

Zoë had been a student in Summerhill. She is first mentioned in a book of Neill's when she was a baby. In the 1980s, when Zoë somewhat reluctantly came back to the school to take it over, she was happily married to a farmer and living just a mile away from the school. She loves horses and she loves animals and she was enjoying life on the farm and looking after her kids.

Once in place as principal it took Zoë a while to figure out what her relationship was going to be with the staff and with the school. The school hit a crucial time in the '90s when Summerhill came under attack from the educational establishment in England. A decision had to be made about how to approach this crisis. Many people were encouraging her to compromise with the government and to capitulate to their demands.

What Zoë eventually decided was, "Yes, we can fix the walls, we can fix the toilets, but when it comes to the philosophy of the school and noncompulsory classes, we are not willing to change and we will fight that right up to the top court in England, and if we fail that, we'll fight it up to the top court in Europe, and if we fail in that, then we will close the school. We will never have a Summerhill School that has compulsory classes." Summerhill won the fight and since that time Zoë and Summerhill seem to be thriving.

A.S. Neill actually owned the school Summerhill outright, so it's a proprietary school, not a non-profit organization. It has been handed down first to his wife and then to his daughter, Zoë.

I've heard some criticism of Summerhill on that basis, as not being truly democratic. You could make a comparison with Sudbury Valley School, for example, which is a non-profit. Their assembly controls it, but actually their assembly is not their meeting. Many other schools use a non-profit board, which is also not the meeting. So in all cases there is actually a legal body, whether an individual owner or a group like a board of trustees, which technically controls the school.

The real question, for whoever manages a school, is to ask to what extent they are empowering the students to make decisions about their own education and about the school. In fact, I don't know if this particular criticism of Summerhill holds up. One of the reasons why Zoë has been adamant about the school not being turned over to a board is she feels that she can actually be more empowered, having total ownership of it, than a board might be.

When Summerhill came under attack by the government, a few years ago, Zoë felt that if there had been a board in place they would have capitulated. They would have caved in to the attack and compromised, rather than taking the government to court and eventually winning the case.

And this was also the basis on which John Potter decided that his school, the New School of Northern Virginia, would be a proprietary school. Maybe it is easier for an individual to totally believe in the empowerment of the students. Maybe that is harder for a committee than an individual.

Summerhill now has over 90 students from ages five to 17. They had an 18 year old last year. They have a timetable of classes that students can choose to go to or not. About 20 of the students are day students and the rest are boarding. A number of the younger kids tend to be day school students whose parents have moved to the area.

They have about a dozen staff members, house parents and teachers who teach in specific areas. The classes are organized by subject, for the most part, and go by a timetable.

Summerhill also has a cleaning staff and a cooking staff that comes in, although some of the students and the teachers are also involved in the cooking and serving process. The meals are delivered regularly at set times.

I think that there always has been a belief at Summerhill that you need to have a stable situation of sleeping arrangements, sleeping times, eating times and so on. That will help establish a secure routine for the kids. They will then have a certain basis for their existence that they can count on. I remember that was also the case at Lewis-Wadhams.

Most things are subject to the school meeting. Changes in bedtimes can be decided. I don't think that the school meeting could decide to, for example, fire all the cooking staff and take over all the cooking themselves. There are certain areas over which Zoë retains power, and one of them is the hiring and firing of staff. And it's also totally her decision whether a kid needs to be kicked out of the school.

Summerhill has just recently changed the way it manages its meetings. This happened in 2002, ironically, when it got to be bigger, when it went from about 60 or 70 students to 90 students. They don't have a tribunal to deal with issues of bullying and stealing anymore. They have a short meeting three times a week and everything goes through that meeting and anything can be put on the agenda.

It was interesting to see that a long-established school like Summerhill was able to change the way they did something so central to the life of the school.

Summerhill also has a system of ombudsmen, people who volunteer to intervene in disputes with younger kids or other people, and act as witnesses at a future meeting if an issue can't be sorted out on the spot.

Neill thought that democracy only worked at boarding schools, but I disagree. I think democracy can work in a lot of different settings, as I've said before. Maybe what he meant is that democracy is most effective in a boarding situation, and I'm not sure that I would disagree with him there. At my school there were times when I wondered why we had day school students. The progress that the day school students made was so much more grudging than the progress the boarding students made, in terms of becoming self-confident, becoming leaders in the school, and all kinds of growth.

Of course, Shaker Mountain's boarding kids had 24 hours a day of the process, including their own democratic meetings as well as the school's. They had a fairly consistent group of people around them who believed in their empowerment.

But for kids at a day school, it's hit or miss when they go home whether or not their parents fully support this approach or even counteract it. Then of course there are deeper questions about the nature of the family setup in our culture. Few families have, for example, family meetings to make decisions.

So I understand what Neill was thinking about. On the other hand if you have a group of like-minded families that want to get together and set up a home school resource center or something like that, it can be quite effective. Creating a community is the essential thing.

After the publication of *Summerhill* there was an explosion in the creation of free schools that continued for over a decade. The average life of a new free school was about 18 months. But some of them are still around, such as Clonlara, in Michigan and Sudbury Valley School in Massachusetts (both founded in 1967), Albany Free School in New York (1969) and The Grassroots Free School in Florida (1972).

As the number of free schools declined, the alternative school movement was born in the public schools. The first ones were for any interested students, and are now called "choice" public alternatives. School Within a School in Brookline, Massachusetts (1971), City as School in New York City (1971), and Alternative Community School in Ithaca, New York (1974). These are all examples which continue into the 21st century. The New Orleans Free School started as a private free school but uniquely became a public magnet school and has survived many attempts to close it down.

In the late 70's and early 80's, under the guidance of John Holt, parents around the United States began homeschooling their children in large numbers. Holt had been a long-term school critic and promoter of alternative schools. He eventually wrote *Teach Your Own,* and rejected the concept of school altogether.

There are now an estimated two million homeschoolers in the United States, and the movement has spread to other countries. For example there are about 100,000 now in England.

In 1991, Joe Nathan's group started the first Charter School in Minnesota. Joe had visited us at Shaker Mountain several years earlier when he was studying Vermont's voucher system. This first charter launched the charter school movement, again inspired by a desire to make education more relevant and learner centered. There are over 2500 charter schools in 2003.

People continue to be dissatisfied with the traditional, standardized, top-down approach of the traditional system. The movement continues. Our work is not done yet.

Chapter Ten
Democratic Schools

I haven't visited Sudbury Valley School in a long time. Sudbury Valley is now the most important democratic school in America, inspiring many people to start schools based on their model. They have a resource pack for people who want to start new schools based on their model that has proven its effectiveness, and they publish many of their own books. Sudbury Valley has pioneered a process of self-examination that is providing us with our first scientific evidence about what happens to kids who grow up in a democratic school. A visit to their web site can really give you the best introduction to their unique way of doing things.

A while back they decided to grow bigger and they now have 250 students. There was a feeling that their kids could benefit from a large number of peers at every age level. My concern is that I don't know how you can ever have a really good democracy with such large numbers. The room that they meet in isn't very large. From what I understand if they ever need to have a meeting with everybody there they have to go out to their barn.

The community at Sudbury Valley has control over every aspect of school life. Their meetings are more formal than the Summerhill meetings or than our meetings at Shaker Mountain were. When I was at Sudbury Valley the people did not sit in a circle, but in rows of chairs, sort of the way a New England town meeting operates. They use Robert's Rules of Order to manage their meetings. My only worry about their meetings is that the process might be too adult-oriented and somewhat discouraging to younger kids who want be involved. But I don't think I can really say that without having seen more meetings.

Sudbury Valley has a judicial committee that meets every school day to deal with people who are accused of various infractions. I sat in on one of these. Students come in and are questioned by members of the committee and the committee votes on what they think the consequences should be or whether they agree that the school law was broken or not. Summerhill used a similar system for a while in the 1930s. At Sudbury Valley the meeting makes the laws and there is an appeal process. Morley Safer recently did quite an effective bit about Sudbury Valley on "60 Minutes."

Now I'm going to tell you about some of the other democratic schools in America that are not as well known as Sudbury Valley:

******

Grassroots Free School, in Tallahassee, Florida, has a meeting they call a "powwow." Although the founder, Pat Seery, spent some time at Summerhill, the school is also influenced by Indian decision-making methods. They have non-compulsory class attendance. I have visited them in two locations.

They are now located within an intentional community, which they established. They moved a former African American church and a couple of other buildings to the property for the school. Seery lives in a house next door in the intentional community.

I think the original thought was that a number of parents living in the intentional community that was surrounding it would have kids going to the school. That is not really the case anymore, which creates an interesting situation. It's funny how these things happen.

Grassroots can keep kids from kindergarten through high school, but generally when kids get to be high school age they don't stay there. Some do, but for the most part they seem to go on to SAIL School, which is a public alternative that Seery helped to establish. One of the impressive things about Seery is that he has always encouraged anybody in the Tallahassee area who wanted to start an alternative to do so and has felt that his school would still survive somehow. He helped start SAIL School and one or two others. Recently, he even hosted the initial meetings to help establish a charter school in the area.

One day I visited and all of the staff had the flu. It struck me that there was really almost no difference between how the school was running with no staff and how it ran with staff. The students organized their various clubs and groups. Recreational games were organized. Kids were working in the library and in classrooms on different projects. They were not at all dependent on the staff organizing things for them. Anyone at Grassroots can call a powwow anytime they want, but I don't know if meetings are regularly scheduled.

******

The Greenbrier School was established as a day school on a large piece of property about 45 minutes from Austin, Texas. The school used to take a bus into Austin, pick up kids, bring them to the school, have school, and bus them home. Gradually people began to come out to the land and build structures on the land to live in. At a certain point, they stopped sending the bus out.

Greenbrier has had up to 100 students but the last time I visited there were maybe 50 people living in the community and 25 kids. The way it has evolved, it's almost like a giant home school. Everybody is there for the kids.

It is still legally a school, not just a community, and it is accredited. Nowadays they occasionally have kids come in as day school students, but generally speaking everybody in the school lives there. I saw wonderful scenes in people's houses, all kinds of classes and one-on-one's with adults. Somebody would be doing a book report in one corner and someone else would be doing driver's education in another.

They used to have a sauna in a meeting building, which burned down. They have a shop, a trampoline and a swimming pool. They do have a main school building, but things can take place anywhere in the community.

In fact, they think of themselves as somewhat of an anarchist community. They all get together and make decisions democratically. Everyone who lives there gets to be involved in the decision-making. As far as I know, no outside teachers are hired. They've been around since the early '70s. One side note: Dave Lehman, one of the premier public educators, currently principal of Alternative Community School in Ithaca, NY, was one of the founders of Greenbrier.

******

The Meeting School, in New Hampshire, predates the free school movement in America by about 10 years. The first director was George Bliss. I met him when the school was in its fifth or sixth year and going nicely. He told me that they'd planned it as a 10-year experiment. The school was to be closed at the end of 10 years, which sounded like a shame. It wasn't closed after 10 years. The school continues today.

It has a Quaker philosophy, but it is at the radical end of Quakerism. The school is experiential in its approach. Their process is consensus and they are clear about which kinds of things kids can and can't make decisions about.

There was a time when the school got down to 14 kids and they were close to closing. This was in the late 1990's. Now, as I understand it, the school is pretty much full. It has over 30 students. Each group of students lives in one of the houses on their campus and has some responsibility for the maintenance of that house.

It's a high school, mostly 10th through 12th grade, and kids are required to go to classes. But it's one of the places I usually recommend first for people who are looking for an alternative boarding school for a high-school-age student. It's in a rural area, in a nice location, and they have barns and many different outbuildings and animals. They try to grow almost all the food that they eat.

******

The same is true of the Arthur Morgan School, a somewhat older school. It was founded by the daughter-in-law of Arthur Morgan, the man who had started the progressive Antioch School in the early 1920s. Later he had been instrumental in radicalizing Antioch College. Arthur's son, Ernest Morgan, died on October 29, 2000, in his nineties. He had helped keep the school going for all these years.

The Arthur Morgan School is the only boarding alternative junior high school in the country. No other group seems to be foolish enough to try to tackle that age, and only that age.

The school has 500 acres in an extremely beautiful area in Burnsville, North Carolina. Like the Meeting School, they make decisions by consensus and have required class attendance. The kids get to do a fair amount of traveling. They have had major field trips where they have gone and worked, for example, in migratory worker camps. These are two good examples of schools outliving their original founders and thriving.

******

Harmony School is in Bloomington, Indiana. Some of the founders of the school are still there, including Steve Bonchek. The school was founded in 1974. It kept moving until about 15 years ago when Steve negotiated an arrangement with the local public school. They were able to buy a former public school building for a symbolic $10. The story they tell is that every kid who planned to be going to the school came in with a dime. At the time there were about 100 kids.

There are 200 or so in the school now. One of the special things about this school is that they do a lot of local fundraising and so even though it's a private school, they have a sliding scale and will take in kids regardless of how little money their family has.

They do have compulsory class attendance, but they also have a democratic meeting. I went there one time and I had quite a debate with the students about whether or not they should have compulsory classes. One kid said to me, "Well, if I didn't have to go to class I would just sit home watching television and smoking all day." I remember his teachers being shocked at that statement—to think that their students really thought that if they were not forced to go to classes they wouldn't be going! But the kids certainly seem to love the school. It's a K-12 school and they take quite an interesting variety of students. I don't know what the limitations of the meeting are.

Harmony School has actually become a hub for some other projects that are related to democratic education. They do consulting at other schools. Daniel Baron, one of the staff members, runs a program in which he goes into other schools around the country and helps them with democratic process. They recently won an award for their process of empowering students democratically.

******

Liberty School, in Blue Hill, Maine, was founded on the 1990's by Arnold Greenberg. Arnold has been a pioneer in alternative education for many years. He helped design the Upper School at Miquon, in Pennsylvania, which is now called Crefeld. He moved up to Maine and became a baker and started a bakery and did some other things.

For some reason he decided to get back into education and take advantage of a law that exists in Maine and Vermont that is a variation on a voucher law. The law says that if your local district or town does not have an official high school then the people in that town can use that money as a voucher to pay for any high school they want.

This came about because in some northern New England towns there was a pre-existing private academy, so that when the public school system came in they worked out a deal to pay those private academies tuition. This, however, has left the law open for about one third of the towns in Vermont and Maine.

Arnold happened to live in an area that was surrounded by four voucher towns. He decided to go into competition with the local academy, organized Liberty School, and found a building company that was willing to put up a building for them with no money down. The idea was that the voucher money would be able to pay off the cost of the building, which is how they were able to start with very little money.

Liberty School right now must be six or seven years old. It's a high school with over 60 students. They have a democratic decision-making process and they do experiential work. They also have a classical music program headed up by a professional musician. That's unique: I don't know of any other democratic school that has a classical music program as part of it.

The kids love the school. They can decide almost anything about the curriculum and about the basic rules of the school. They are expected to go to class and the kids are serious about their academics. It is unique, too, in that it really is one of very few democratic voucher schools. It shows how this kind of thing could work. They recently received a major grant so they can build upon the work they have pioneered.

******

Jefferson County Open School is one of the more interesting public alternatives in the US, founded by Arnie Langberg. He had started a public alternative on Long Island before he went out to the Denver area. First, in Denver, he started a program called Mountain Open, then another program for younger kids called Tanglewood. These programs were later merged into the Jefferson County Open School.

The setup for the older kids still seems radical. They encourage their students to go anywhere they would like to go. When I was there I heard a report from a group of kids about a canoe trip they had made up in Canada. There was also a girl who had gone down to a biological research laboratory in Louisiana.

They have a democratic process for their 600 kids and a democratic meeting for the older kids. They use a system of advisory groups. Each kid has an advisor, who meets with them individually but also in a group setting.

The last time I visited was the day of the Columbine massacre. A number of us had gone to a conference of the National Coalition of Alternative Community Schools that was held near Denver, where Jefferson County is.

By prearrangement, the students from the Albany Free School had planned to stay in the Jefferson County gym. At that point, all the other schools in Denver were closed as a result of the massacre and people were very worried about the situation. Out of concern for their security our kids were actually locked in the building and there were guards around. If they wanted to leave the building for any purpose they had to contact the security people and let them know that the door was going to be opened.

I interviewed Arnie Langberg on my national radio show the night of Columbine and I talked to him about his school and the nearby Columbine High School, which actually had a number of former Jefferson County students going there at the time. I asked him if something like this could have happened in his school and he said no, they might have had a couple of kids that were that crazy, but because of the degree and depth of communication in his school, they would find out about it. Arnie felt that this kind of thing could not have happened at Jefferson County because people would have gone to see what these kids were up to.

******

Another interesting public school is The Met, in Providence, Rhode Island. One of the founders is Dennis Littky. His partner is Eliot Washor. Dennis has been a longtime public school gadfly. He's been fighting the system forever.

He was able to start this school in Providence, technically under the vocational school system, as part of the regular public school system. The idea of these vocational schools is that the maximum number of students is 100 and the emphasis is on internships. There seems to be a pretty good mixture of kids.

A lot of the students' time is spent in internships, working in a field that interests them. They come into the school at various times during the week and work with multi-age advisory groups. Each student has an individual learning plan. They have a general meeting every week, one of which I sat in on. Their meeting starts with a group activity; they will sometimes have a speaker talk at the meeting, and they make decisions about the program.

When I went to the school, a couple of students were doing a presentation on a project they had organized, in which they had gone down south doing research on the civil rights movement. They saw where Martin Luther King was killed, and they had gotten to meet James Meredith, who first integrated the schools down there.

The group had to do their own fundraising to be able to make the trip. They made a connection with a group from a college nearby and went on the tour with them. I watched their joint presentation with representatives from the college group, to parents, staff, and other students.

They put on a slide show and showed videos and it seemed an impressive project and a good example of some of the kinds of things that they're able to do at the Met. The Met now has funding from the Gates Foundation. As a result of the success of this first school, the directors have opened three more in Providence and are opening at least eight more in Providence and in other cities around the country. The book about the Met, called *One Kid at a Time*, was written by Eliot Levine, and is a good description of how the school works.

******

North Star Center, which used to be called Pathfinder Learning Center, is in Hadley, Massachusetts. It was originally the idea of Josh Hornick and Ken Danford. They tried to get funding for a radical charter school in which kids would have a lot of freedom to study what they wanted. Their proposal for a charter school was not funded so they decided to set this up as an educational program for home schoolers instead.

The idea originally was that kids could come in anytime they wanted and classes would be organized for them. Since they were home schoolers, no set curriculum was imposed. The basic educational responsibility was still taken by the parents. After a while the home schoolers kind of drifted away and then people started contacting North Star, saying they wanted their kids to go to the school.

The staff pointed out that it was not a school and that for kids to go there they would have to become home schoolers. Josh estimates that maybe 85 percent of the kids going there now are from families who came to them originally and had to be helped through the process of becoming home schoolers. They usually have somewhere around 40 students.

When I visited them the last time they were in a very pleasant space but they have since moved to another one. They have meetings of all the kids and they have classes that are scheduled. Students can also ask for classes if they want or they can hang out with each other. It is an opportunity for kids who are technically home schooling to be able to socialize and to have control of their education.

I think this is significant for a number of reasons: This is a way that home schooling can grow beyond the usual model of a parent teaching their kids at home. Parents, when they're home schooling, have the right to hire whoever they want to do the teaching of their kids even though they still take the legal responsibility.

The current homeschool system is limited mostly to two parent families in which one can stay at home, or to people who have home businesses. It can expand from that if parents start using home school resource centers. A number of similar centers are popping up all around the United States.

Chapter Eleven
Public Alternatives

People can say that kids in alternative schools don't get to experience being in a public school classroom (with 47 other kids) and are missing out. Well, I think that people in public schools are having a very unreal experience because a lot of what is going on there is not related to the reality of the students. But alternative schools can have their own problems.

Alternative schools that pretend to be democratic can be worse than traditional schools. It is dangerous to imply that the kids are empowered to do things that they're not really empowered to do. It is dangerous to try to fool them or lead them on or manipulate them.

I remember having a discussion with David Greenberg, the son of Sudbury Valley School founders Daniel and Hannah Greenburg. David was at that time a 15-year-old student at Sudbury Valley. (Now he is an adult and a founder of another Sudbury-based school). He was talking about schools that are not democratic but are still very nice and give the kids some freedom. David said he would rather be in a military school than be in a school in which people are nice and smiley and happy and friendly but had compulsory classes. He said he'd rather know who his true enemies were.

I do agree with that sentiment. Almost any institution can have a democratic process, as long as students aren't misled into believing they have more power than they do. It just has to be absolutely clear what decisions the kids are allowed to make and which ones they're not able to make and who then is making those decisions.

To have a full-scale democratic system you have to have the authority to empower people. Or you can do something like what John Gatto did in what he called his "guerrilla curriculum"; that is, you decide as a teacher that you need to become like a spy and go underground and try to empower students to make decisions, even though you know you're not allowed to empower them to make those decisions. Some teachers have done this; sometimes it has worked and sometimes they have gotten fired.

I know that John Gatto used to try to sneak the kids out of the classroom and into the community to do experiential projects and then cover for them. That's one way of doing it. But generally speaking, you need to have authority that you can actually give to students to make decisions. That's a first requirement. Beyond that you have to have educators that believe that students have the right to make these decisions and that the decisions will be better than if they were made arbitrarily by an administration. If you don't have that basic belief in your bones, then I don't know how you can do it.

There is an intrinsic problem with using democratic systems in public school classrooms. The system, being an authoritarian system, gives a lot of arbitrary power to the teacher. These schools tend to attract people who are authoritarian and who like to have that power. They don't want to empower students and listen to them. The majority of people in the public school system have that trait to some extent, and that militates against the system ever becoming empowering. It's one of the self-perpetuating aspects of the system.

You might be able to determine to what extent people are authoritarian in their orientation by the way they answer certain questions. This could be the basis of some interesting research. I do know that people who have done research on different learning styles have discovered that the learning style of most teachers is fairly different from the learning styles of their students. In fact it is different from kids who wind up in the at-risk public alternative schools. Many of those kids are experiential learners and many of the teachers who have been successful in the system are auditory people who learn best by sitting in a classroom and listening to what people say.

A lot of the problems with public schools go back to the roots of the public education system. In fact, John Gatto has documented this in his books. The system was not really designed to democratize or to teach democracy or to get people ready to function in a democratic society. The roots of the system were more to do with certain political agendas when the system was created.

For example, a lot of Protestants in the United States, the majority at the time, were very much afraid of the influx of Catholics who were pouring into the country in the 1800s and so they wanted to Protestantize them. That was one of the motivations for the public school system.

Another one was to get people ready to work in factories because we were in the middle of the industrial revolution. They wanted people to be prepared to follow orders, to change what they were doing at the sound of a bell. All of those things were not conducive to encouraging a democratic or open society. They came from a political agenda. What we have today is really the logical extension of a system that had those roots.

Of course, who is to say this isn't still the political agenda of some people in power? Naturally it's easier for the people in charge if they are not being questioned or challenged. It makes it easier for them to do the things they want to do.

We don't have a whole lot of political leaders who really want to empower people democratically, and who want to come up with creative ideas and get the input of constituents. Maybe that's because they are all people who came out of our undemocratic educational system. In fact, this could be another reason why we don't have lots of democratic schools. It is certainly one of the reasons why it is such an uphill fight to create them.

In most schools no significant decisions are made by the students. This is partly because the people in charge don't want students to recognize that they might have the right to make significant decisions. Also, it would just make things more complicated and more difficult for the administrators. The simplest thing, of course, is to have an authoritarian system in which the people in the administration make all the decisions.

Public schools could begin to have some effective democracy, even if the decisions were limited to certain specific areas. But to make the transition in a public school system is difficult because the public school system is set up everywhere as an authoritarian system, with various levels of power and decision-making authority. I don't know of a single school district anywhere in the United States in which decisions are made democratically and involve students. There are individual programs and individual schools but I don't know of any place where there's a whole district.

Real change has to happen on at least a district level. Otherwise what will need to happen, and what does seem to be happening, is for millions of people simply to go around the system. They will have to opt out. This is now more hopeful than anything happening within the system.

I was thinking about an inefficient dam holding back a lot of water. First, all the water goes around the outside. After a while cracks develop in the middle. If you want to break down the dam, you have to hope that the breach, happening from the inside, will get wider and wider. Maybe you have to have some kind of internal change happening also. It's an interesting analogy, but unfortunately analogies don't always necessarily coincide with reality.

I just don't know that there is any easy answer to it. At one point I thought that what was happening in District 4 in New York City was going to be precedent setting.

At that time Debbie Meier was in this district, up in Spanish Harlem. It was the lowest scoring district of the 32 districts in New York City on almost any standardized tests. The superintendent gave Debbie a school to do what she wanted with, to see if she could do something different. She then set up the Central Park East alternative school.

This was a school in which the kids could learn in a relaxed environment. The teachers were empowered to make a lot of decisions about how they wanted to teach. The kids could wander around the building, they could work on the floor, and so on. It was so effective that they immediately set up Central Park East 2 and started a process by which they eventually created a lot of alternative schools within this district. Then they waited until some big schools failed, or almost failed, and broke them up into smaller schools within their old buildings.

Eventually they had 55 schools in 20 buildings. It seemed terribly exciting. The average reading score in that district went from the bottom to the middle and they even began to have more white kids coming into the district, than leaving it, every day. In Spanish Harlem!

Unfortunately these ideas didn't spread to other districts. I always thought that once they demonstrated the effectiveness of these ideas, maybe other districts in New York City would start moving in the same direction. But that didn't happen. There were only a few other alternative schools established around New York City.

One of the interesting things was that Debbie Meier's model empowered teachers but it didn't empower students. I remember having a discussion with Debbie about this and she said she didn't want to have a democratic decision-making process or have meetings in these schools that would end up being phony. So, rather than have one that was phony, like a student council, she wasn't going to have anything and she never did have anything.

Her focus was on teacher empowerment, which was in itself a problem in the city. That is the basis on which the alternative schools that exist in New York City have been established and therefore to my knowledge there is not actually any democratic school in New York City.

There are some alternatives, some things that are more learner-centered, experiential, and so on, in the city. There are some terrific public alternatives such as City as School, a public high school with 500 kids in it, in which the student's curriculum consists of internships in their fields of interest around the city. And there are some other ones with their own unique aspects; however, there are no actual democratic public schools that specifically empower students to make decisions about their school in the city.

It also happens that there are currently no private alternatives that I know of that are democratic in New York City. The actor Orson Bean established the 15th Street School in the 1960s. That democratic school ran for a long time, but has since closed.

Meanwhile, Debbie Meier herself got frustrated with working in the city and has now gone to direct the Mission Hill Elementary School in Boston. One of the things that is interesting about her experience is that it shows how one school's ideas can at least spread to a district.

It also shows how difficult it is to put cracks in that dam.

Chapter Twelve
Crimea and the Ukraine

Back in 1991, I got a letter in the mail from Ron Miller announcing the first New Schools Festival of the Soviet Union. He said he couldn't go and wondered if I might be interested in going. At that point, the idea seemed completely preposterous.

I didn't know anything about the Soviet Union; it seemed like a forbidding place. Nobody really knew that there had been any kind of new or alternative schools in Russia. But the more I thought about it the more I realized that our new organization, the Alternative Education Research Organization (AERO) should be doing just this kind of thing. We should be finding out about various kinds of alternatives that were out there and connecting people.

I got in touch with the woman in Holland, Uta Roehl, who was dealing with the festival-goers from Europe. At this time the only American who was going was Albert Lamb, who was working in England at Summerhill. Ute informed me about the rather complicated logistics that were involved. I had to get formal invitations, visas, and arrange transportation.

Around the same time I was contacted by a home schooler in Virginia who had done some traveling with me. His name was Noah. I told him about the possibility of this trip and he was excited about doing it.

I talked to his family and warned them that there could be some dangers involved, and that it was a completely unknown thing to me. But they had confidence that we would be okay. Then I had some conversations with Noah on just how we wanted to get there and we settled on the idea that we didn't want to drop out of the sky into Russia. We decided that we would fly to England and then take a train to Russia.

We got our visas, flew to England, took the ferry to Belgium, and the next day we got on a train called the East West Express. It consisted of several cars that they would continue to attach and detach to one train or another until it got to Moscow. The East West Express was not fancy and few people on it spoke English.

We brought some food with us, but we didn't realize that we probably should have brought a lot of food with us. There was no diner on the train. At one point I heard that on one of the cars behind us there was a man who had come on with a pushcart with food on it, several cars back. So I walked back to find this guy and was able to pick up some drinks and food.

When I got back to our car, the door was locked going from one carriage to the other. I looked out through the window. We had stopped at a station platform. Our car, with Noah in it, was separating from my stationary carriage and was pulling ahead. I jumped out of that train and ran down the platform and caught up with our train, just managing to jump in the last door. Otherwise, Noah would have been going to Russia on his own.

When we got to the border of Poland, to what was then the edge of the Soviet Union, the size of the tracks changed. We figured that the logical thing would be to have us change trains. That was not what happened. Instead, they jacked up the cars and changed all the wheels on the entire train to adapt to the different size of the tracks.

I was told that Stalin had made the tracks smaller on purpose, so he couldn't be attacked easily by train. I managed to videotape a little of this process until they came over and practically knocked the camera out of my hands.

We continued on to Moscow and met Alexander Tubelsky, from the School of Self-Determination, and he showed us around Moscow. Then we got on another train and went down through Harkov and the Ukraine, where my mother's mother was born, and into the Crimea to a town by the name of Semiferipole. The Crimea was the Florida of the Soviet Union. It was where everyone went to get to the ocean, which in this case was the Black Sea. This was now August and it was very warm.

There were 400 people at this conference and 70 kids. The organizers understood that in order to have a good festival of New Schools, they needed to have the students there. It was a wonderful conference; I made all kinds of connections that continue to this day. As a result of that conference, communication was opened up between alternative schools in the former Soviet Union and the west. I met Alexander Adamsky and Elina Shepel who were from the Eureka Free University and were doing a teacher-training program to train teachers in alternative methods of education. I subsequently went to several of their training sessions with groups of people from the west.

And this is where I met people from the Stork Family School. Their school is in a town called Vinnitsa in the Ukraine. When they met me and discovered that my grandmother was born in the Ukraine, they considered me American only by accident of birth, and they adopted me into their family. I made a connection with the Stork School that couldn't be broken.

They even had me participate in a play they were putting on. It was kind of a political play based on *The Goose That Laid the Golden Egg.* They gave me some lines to memorize in Russian and when I spoke those lines, it brought down the house.

After the conference we went back to Moscow. At the station they wouldn't let us get on the train to go back to England because we hadn't reserved our ticket on a specific day. We told them that we had been down in the Crimea and hadn't been able to do that. They said that maybe if we went down the next day and got in line, we might be able to book a ticket.

The next day we did just that, but we weren't able to get tickets, so I said to Noah, "Well, we're going to do this the American way. Let's go see the boss." Our translator came with us and we went to see the head of the railroad at the Moscow station. He said there was nothing he could do. We would need to give him several days' notice.

I told the railroad boss that we were having a meeting later that day in Vice-President Boris Yeltsin's White House. He said, "In that case, we can put you first on the waiting list but you will still have to call us later."

So we called the boss later from Yeltsin's White House. He said we should go down and get the tickets immediately. The White House dispatched a car for us, brought us to the station, and we got the tickets. The next day we got on the train and headed off to England.

Forty-five hours later, when we got to England, we discovered that where we had been standing around in front of the Russian White House, just two day before, was where Yeltsin wound up, standing up on a tank, to hold off the army troops attempting their failed coup.

Not long after that that there was no more Soviet Union. Then Yeltsin became the president of whatever was left of the Soviet Union.

In the following years I went to several conferences that were organized by Eureka Free University in Russia and the Stork School was also invited to a couple of them. So I continued to see the wonderful relationship that the students had with the teachers. A deep level of communication existed between them and they worked closely together at these conferences.

AERO had continued to maintain a relationship with them all through those years but I had never actually been to the school until 1998, when we did the International Democratic Education Conference at the Stork Family School in Vinnitsa, Ukraine. During the years when they had financial crises, we were able to get funds to help them survive. At one point, the government was taking something like 80 percent of their tuition in taxes. They obviously were trying to discourage the existence of a private school. Finally, in January of 2001, I was invited to participate in the 10th anniversary celebration of the Stork School.

The school moved to its present location in a former state kindergarten several years ago. It is a sizable two-floor building. Now they have about 200 students, kindergarten through 12th Grade. They are divided up into different age and class levels. The school is broadly based in terms of arts and music and academics. They don't have a democratic process for the whole school, but they have done some experimenting with it, after learning more about it, and some of the individual classes may now have a democratic process.

The kids seem to love being there. They have a special museum, where a craftsman teaches the kids how to do pottery work and clay work. They do weaving. They learn all kinds of music with an amazing music teacher who teaches them songs in many different languages. They learn to play different instruments and they seem also to do very well in things like science and math. One of the graduates is currently at the Russian equivalent of MIT.

Something they do that is unique is that they have a Montessori program option for younger kids at the school. I don't know that I've ever seen another school that had a choice for parents of a Montessori or non-Montessori program for the kids.

They first heard about Montessori at that original first New Schools festival. At that point there were no Montessori schools in all of the Soviet Union. That's just one example of the kind of flexibility that the Stork School has.

It's hard to communicate the depth of caring of these people, the depth of their humanity, and their commitment to the school and to the kids who are in the school. They've survived against incredible odds to keep the school going and it is a very bright light.

Recently they were selected to host the UNESCO Conference. I think people are beginning to notice this school and how special it is.

Chapter Thirteen
Alternative Thinkers

John Holt was one of the leading writers of our movement. He wrote effective critiques of conventional education and encouraged people to start alternative schools. He had been writing books on education since the early 1960s, including his bestseller *How Children Fail* and its companion, *How Children Learn.* In the late '70s he gave up on the idea of schools and wrote a book called *Teach Your Own.* That was one of the beginnings of the home school movement, growing out of the alternative school movement.

I first met John Holt around 1967. I was not in school anymore, but I met him when he was speaking at Goddard College. I was teaching at one of the regular schools I taught at before I started Shaker Mountain. After his talk I said to him that I wanted to get a job at an alternative school somewhere. So he took down some information about me.

Not long after that, I got a letter from John Holt asking me if I had found an alternative school to teach in. This to me was amazing, that he would follow up on all of these things. I wrote back to him and told him I had started a school, whereupon John Holt immediately put us on his list of endorsed alternative schools. This was very important to us because we then had all kinds of people who knew about us and who would contact us, wanting to teach at the school or support it. This started a communication I had with John over a long period of time. At that point he was still in his mode of being critical of schools and promoting alternative education.

Whenever I would get down to the Boston area I would stop by and visit him.

After a while he soured on the whole idea of schools and started his "Growing Without Schooling" magazine, which led to the *Teach Your Own* book. I stopped in his office and had a discussion with him there and he was skeptical that any kids would want to go to any school if they weren't forced to go. It was difficult to convince him that Shaker Mountain was exceptional, that this was a school in which kids were not required to go to classes and in which they tried to have school even when we had vacations. He did allow the possibility that such a school could exist, a school that kids would want to go to even if they weren't forced.

Later on when I was working as director of Mayor Bernie Sanders' Children and Youth Committee, we invited John Holt to come to Vermont as a speaker at the local auditorium, co-hosted by Shaker Mountain School and the mayor's office. We invited alternative schools and home schoolers from all over the state to come and John drew quite a big audience. Out of this we put together the first organization for home schoolers in Vermont.

John stayed overnight at our emergency shelter in Burlington. He was staying in our best room, which was the director's room, and that's where the phone was. At one point the phone rang and it was a kid who had run away but wanted to come back. We were talking to him on the phone and started to take the phone out of the room and John sat straight up and said, "Oh no, please don't take the phone out of the room!" He wanted to hear the whole conversation and was very interested in what we were doing. Of course, the boy did come back. We didn't have many who ran away from that shelter.

I saw John for the last time, before his early death, when he spoke at the NCACS Conference in 1985 at Clonlara School in Michigan.

Someone asked him a question about the problems of fundamentalist Christian home schoolers who try to do a kind of rigid school at home. He said he felt that over time either the kids would teach the parents how to teach them or the parents would give up and just put their kids in a Christian school. I think time has tended to bear that out. Now the whole idea about the line between religious home schooling and unschooling and so on is blurred. There are many religious home schoolers that liberally quote John Holt and are basically unschoolers. His prediction in that respect was accurate.

I do occasionally think about John Holt and the way he did his work as being in some ways a role model for what we're doing at AERO. Our vision and goal always has been that if we could really unite this movement, we could have a significant impact on the education system and move the whole system in the direction of a learner-centered approach, one that really respected the needs and the rights of students.

AERO has the lonely task of trying to get people from these different types of alternatives to be aware of the other alternatives and to provide support and resources to people who are trying to provide a generally learner-centered approach in education. A few other people, besides John Holt, have done similar things; one was Len Solo who played a similar role with his Teacher Dropout Center in Massachusetts. Len Solo went on to run the Cambridge Alternative Public School and then, from 1983 to 2001, Cambridge's Graham and Parks School.

******

Another excellent writer on education was Jonathan Kozol, who had been a substitute teacher in the Boston public schools when he was young. He didn't teach for long but he wrote a book about it, the bestseller *Death at an Early Age* about the life of minority public school kids in the Boston system, and then he continued to write about alternative schools.

Kozol wrote a book called *Free Schools.* One of the lines in his book caught the attention of someone on my staff. It was something to the effect that he cared about schools that worked with poor kids and inner city kids and minority kids and not schools like those out in the country up in Vermont. Alan Boutillier, a Shaker Mountain staff member, wrote to Kozol and said it was time he learned something about schools up in Vermont. Boutillier said that we had a school that worked with mostly low-income kids, and some inner city kids and welfare kids and he said that he took great exception to what he wrote. Kozol wrote back and apologized for that and said he would like to find out more about us. He actually got us a couple of hundred dollars through something called the New Nations Seed Fund.

Then around 1974 he invited me to a meeting in Boston at which they were going to try to create a national organization of alternative schools. There were only a dozen of us who went to that meeting in the basement of a church. Some of the others included Mary Leue of The Free School in Albany, and Dave Lehman, who later was principal at the Alternative Community School in Ithaca. Dave, at the time, was still busy editing the "New Schools Exchange Newsletter," one of the early networking newsletters for alternative schools. My friend Greg

Packan from Shaker Mountain, who was a lawyer, was also there.

We had this long discussion—I remember Kozol was sick; he had the flu or something. At that point he seemed to be espousing a philosophy that was pretty much extreme left in orientation. One of the discussions we had was questioning whether public schools should be allowed into this new coalition. Kozol was very much against it. He thought that public schools were part of a sort of state conspiracy and he kept using words like "proletariat" and so on. Both Mary and I said, "Look, this kind of language isn't going to wash in our communities." We were advocating being more inclusive.

A couple of years later Kozol, with some other people—one of them was Jack Wuest—organized the first National Coalition of Alternative Community Schools meeting. They had quite a turnout and as a result, Jack Wuest eventually set up something called the Alternative Schools Network in Chicago, which continues to this day.

For a couple of years after that meeting there were no more meetings. Pat Montgomery, of Clonlara, started contacting people asking what happened to the NCACS. They resurrected it and had another meeting. This was around 1980. I went to my first NCACS meeting in 1982 in Chicago.

The last time I saw Kozol was at a conference that was organized by Jesse Jackson in Washington, DC in 2000. The opening was at the National Press Corp and he was one of the one or two featured speakers. I talked to him after that and gave him a copy of our magazine. He, of course, has made quite a name for himself over the years writing about children and minorities and the public schools. One of his latest books is called *Savage Inequalities.* I've always thought it was somewhat ironic that he has become the champion of what can be done and what ought to be done for the public school system whereas back in that meeting in the '70's he didn't even want public schools to be part of the coalition he was going to set up.

******

George Dennison was primarily a writer but in New York City he set up a school called The First Street School that had a lot of low-income kids. He wrote a wonderful book called *The Lives of Children* about the way these kids responded to the school situation. That became an important early book in the movement.

In a related story, at this time I had just started my school and there was a local religious ecumenical organization in the same town called BEAM (Burlington Ecumenical Action Ministry). I had gone to them originally to see if I could get their support for Shaker Mountain. We talked about the way we wanted to run the school, the kids who were going to be in it and so on. They expressed quite a bit of interest in what we were doing and the philosophy of it.

I went to them a couple of times for support but I didn't hear from them. Then one day I talked to a kid that I knew in Burlington and she said, "Oh, I've got to go to my free school now."

I said, "Your what?"

And she said, "Yes, yes, we started a new school." It had been started by that same ecumenical organization.

I asked who was in it and it was interesting: they were middle class kids. I contacted them and asked what happened; we had asked them for support and then they had started a school in competition with ours. They said they took what we told them very seriously and called some kids together that they knew to discuss what we had said. Lo and behold, the kids said they wanted something like this too. So rather than contact us and support us and get the kids into our school—with mostly low-income kids—they set up a middle class alternative to what we were doing!

This is a painful lesson that I learned about liberals: these people were oblivious about what they had done. To them, it was all just a natural consequence: they asked the kids and they wanted to do something and there it was. They were totally unconscious about how it might affect our school.

A little later, I heard through the people that I knew that George Dennison was coming to town to see the new free school. So I arranged to be there when he came. I introduced myself to him after his talk and told him about what we were doing and he was very interested. He went out to dinner with us afterwards. He came over to our school and stayed overnight at the boarding part in Starksboro. He said that he was sure that the middle class alternative school couldn't survive; liberals didn't have the guts to pull it off. But he was interested in what we were doing and totally supportive of it.

Some time after that I had a group of kids who went on a trip with me to Maine and Nova Scotia. We were on our way to visit a school in New Brunswick called School in the Barn. It was an early alternative school. On the way we stopped to visit and stayed overnight at George Dennison's house and met his wife Mabel. Not too much later than that he died. We were in touch with Mabel for a long time. She was involved with an alternative school in Maine.

******

Edgar Z. Friedenberg was an important pioneer writer in education and one of his most important books was *The Vanishing Adolescent*. I gather that in protest of the Vietnam War he moved to Canada and he stayed there. I got the sense talking to him that in some respects he regretted that.

I was in communication with him and he invited me to come up to speak at Delhausie University in Halifax, Nova Scotia. This was in the late '70s. I went with two of my students by train to Montreal and from there to Nova Scotia and we stayed with Edgar for a few days. I spoke at his school. His house was a little ways away from Halifax, on the ocean.

He was living alone but he had a husky, a dog by the name of Sespe. Sespe was treated as if he were human by Edgar. He was a very smart dog. He could pick up things that you said just conversationally. For example, if Edgar said, "Well, maybe we'll take a walk out along the beach," in a conversational tone, the dog would jump up and down in excitement because he understood exactly what had been said.

Once when Edgar was out of the house Sespe seemed irritated and upset. We found a little food to try to feed him. He clearly didn't care about the food, didn't want to be petted, and was making strange sounds, kind of whining like wa-wa-wa. After a while, I got the feeling that the dog was actually trying to talk to us. I listened to him one more time and it sounded as if maybe somebody who couldn't speak properly was trying to say, "Where's Edgar?" So I said to the dog, "Did you say, 'Where's Edgar?" And Sespe said, "Wa." I said, "He's gone out to the chalet to do some work." At which point the dog calmly walked over to the door and waited to be let out. We opened the door, and he went down to the chalet.

Someone recently told me that Edgar died within the last two years, and that Sespe also died recently. I'm sorry I never stayed in contact with Edgar because he seemed an interesting and nice guy.

******

Mary Leue was the founder of The Free School of Albany, New York, one of America's oldest and most innovative democratic schools. She started out because she needed something for her own kids who were not happy in school. That grew into what became The Free School. She is, I think, in many ways a genius.

She hasn't been a writer in the same way as these other thinkers, but she has been an important editor. Her quirky and independent "Skole" magazine was for many years a real beacon to the alternative school movement. Mary managed to publish many of the most interesting stories to come out of the recent resurgence of democratic schools. Now she is retired and "Skole" has become a rather different sort of magazine, called "Paths of Learning."

One of her most important early acts, and she says this was very influenced by Jonathan Kozol, was her decision not to try to base the income for the school on tuition but rather to start a business to support it. The business was buying up a bunch of row houses in inner-city Albany and fixing them up. The income they make helps run the school.

The school has always run as a democracy, with quite young children, and the kids have a fair amount of freedom. The Free School has found many unique ways, over the years, to interact with their inner-city community and to create a strong sense of community amongst themselves.

The meetings at The Free School in Albany are called council meetings because they are based on an Indian approach and were not just a pure democracy.

After we got to know each other in the early '70s, we had quite a bit of reciprocal visitation. They would come visit us in Vermont and we'd go down to visit them. We influenced each other. Mary says that the fact that we had a boarding location influenced her to do whatever she could to get the kids out of Albany and over to her farm in the Berkshires, spending some time away from home.

Mary is a strong character, as you have to be to keep something like that going and thriving. She sometimes has a temper and often over the years she would get mad at me and slam down the phone and I would just pick it up and call her back again and we'd continue our conversation. So she knew I wasn't intimidated by her and that's been an important part of our relationship. I consider Mary to be one of my best friends and she's been very helpful to me over the years in a lot of my work.

Mary is now living at her ancestral home in Massachusetts. It's hard for her to be away from The Free School but one of the things I pointed out to her is that it looks as if she organized the school so well that it is one of the few schools that actually seems to have made the transition to the next generation of people and stayed as strong as it's ever been. I think this is something that she really has to be proud of.

Chapter Fourteen
Three More Schools

The School of Self-Determination was started by Alexander Tubelsky as an experimental school in inner-city Moscow. It has always been part of the regular public school system. They currently have 1,200 students from pre-kindergarten through 12th Grade.

The school has a parliament that makes basic decisions about how the school runs. The students have a constitution with specific rights. One of those rights is to leave any class whenever they want without explanation, the same as any adult would be able to do.

When prospective teachers come into the school, they give sample lessons to the students and then the students vote on which teachers are going to be hired. This is the kind of thing that couldn't happen in any public school in the United States that I know of.

Also, within this school, there is a special program called Park Schooling or the Park School, which is based on the ideas of Miloslav Balaban. His daughter, Olga, organized this program within the School of Self-Determination. The 70 students in this program are able to use any of the school facilities as they see fit; for example, they can go teach a class of younger students, they can work in any of the studios they want—woodworking, sewing, weaving, etc.—they can do plays, and they can work independently. This program has been going for five years and has been very successful.

Alexander Tubelsky, who still runs the School of Self-Determination, was a professional actor before he went into education and you can see this by the way he interacts with students. I've brought American students with me to visit his school and when they have been in the same room with Tubelsky, they were fixed in rapt attention as he spoke, just fascinated by the way he expresses himself, even though they couldn't understand a word of Russian.

A good friend of mine, Alla Denesenko, was a teacher in the school and the head of the foreign language department and she worked very closely with Tubelsky in the early years, several years before the coup, when they were setting up this school. It came about as part of Glasnost.

Alla said they went into an existing public school, took it over, and then had to make their radical changes in that school, something that's incredibly difficult to do. Alla talks in detail about the trials and tribulations they went through during this rough period during which the teachers were questioning the approach that Tubelsky was taking with the kids. But now the school runs quite smoothly and, according to Tubelsky, there are at least 16 or 17 other democratic schools now that are part of an association that they have helped to organize.

In their school parliament they elect representatives. It would be pretty much impossible to have a meeting with a school of 1,200 people. Not impossible, but I don't know that they have any place that would hold such a large number. The representatives make the decisions with the teachers. I don't know too much about how it runs because although I've visited the school, I haven't actually seen the parliament.

One concern I have about the school is that Tubelsky subscribes to a view that is common in Russia, something called "Author's Schools." The concept behind them is that these schools are something like works of art by a particular leader. The problem with that concept is that each school is unique and not replicable. However this does go along with my idea that these schools must first be run by charismatic democratic leaders who can empower students.

******

When I first visited the Democratic School of Hadera, they were hosting the International Democratic Education Conference there. They have 300 students and at the time they had 3000 on their waiting list. It's in Hadera, Israel, north of Tel Aviv in a big open campus area with a bunch of buildings in a square with a great big open area in the middle. They have classrooms, a library, music room, art rooms, outside play equipment for the kids and so on. It's a kindergarten through 12th grade school.

What disturbed me a lot about the situation when I first visited is that home schooling is illegal in Israel, or was at the time. With so many on the waiting list it seemed almost unconscionable that the ones that couldn't go there couldn't be home schooling. This has been somewhat rectified by the person who was then the director of the school, Yaacov Hecht. He has established over 20 new democratic schools with government money, since that time, and more are being established.

Yaacov is an amazingly dynamic man who has a clear vision of kids being natural learners. He describes himself as a dyslexic and is very self-deprecating when he talks. But he's a brilliant speaker.

There is a parliament at the school that makes decisions, but again, it seems that the room for the parliament is hardly big enough for 300 people to sit in there so I wonder what happens when they have a really hot issue. They also have some kind of separate judicial system for people who break the rules of the school. The staff lean toward the Sudbury model of having no scheduled classes, but they have a vote about this every year and every year the students vote that they want to have scheduled classes. So that's the way it seems to continue.

There have been quite an interesting variety of schools established that have been modeled from the Democratic School of Hadera. One of them was just started recently by Moshe Lerner. It combines religious and non-religious students and it's quite innovative.

Few schools in Israel bring Jews and Arabs together, but there is one wonderful school that Yaacov describes that is in a very poor area of Tel Aviv. They have a large building so they were able to do some innovative things. They have about one third fairly poor Jewish families who couldn't afford to move out of the area, one third Arabs, and about one third foreign workers who have come into the country. It used to have the very lowest test scores in all of Tel Aviv.

They have made the school experiential. They brought in a number of interesting people who now have workshops or offices in the school building, on the condition that they provide learning experiences and internships for the students in the school. They even have a circus that has its home base in the basement. There are legal offices and craftsmen who operate out of the school. All of these people provide learning experiences for the kids.

A survey was done of all the schools around Tel Aviv and the kids that liked their school the most were the kids from this school. They also had the greatest jump in their rate of learning of any school in the city, according to the standardized tests. There is also a democratic school in the Golan Heights and several others around the country.

One interesting experiment that Yaacov is working on is taking an entire town of 5000 people in the desert and making it into a learning community. Everyone living there is available educationally to other people in the community. This has been so successful that the town is actually growing very rapidly. I think it will have a population of 10,000 sometime soon because a lot of people from different parts of Israel are moving in.

These innovations that have grown out of the Democratic School of Hadera, and are continuing to be fomented by Yaacov Hecht, are certainly impressive. Another thing that Yaacov is creating is a university for training people to teach in these democratic schools.

******

Sands School is in Ashburton, a small town in the beautiful English coastal county of Devon. Three teachers who had worked together at Dartington Hall started it. Dartington was one of the oldest and most famous radical boarding schools in England. When it closed, about 15 or so years ago, three of the staff members, David Gribble, Sybilla Higgs and Sean Bellamy, got together to set up a day school, Sands.

Sands is in a big old house with couple of acres of land behind it, right on the main street that goes through Ashburton. A block away is a swimming pool and they have tennis and basketball courts in the backyard. There are some gardens and a climbing wall. They have one outbuilding that is an art building and another one that is for woodworking. Seventy kids are attending now, which is about as big as it's been. When I visited at first it had only about 35 kids and they were worrying about whether the school could be sustained.

Sands runs as a democracy with non-compulsory class attendance. One of the significant things about Sands is that it's a day school. So whereas Summerhill can draw its kids from all over the world, Sands has to find its kids locally. They seem to have been able to do that, and also some people have moved to the area so their kids could go to the school. They even have a few kids who are living with other families so that they can attend. Students' ages range from 11 to 16.

Sands School has an admissions committee that decides who can get in. I've sat in on one admissions committee meeting, which was comprised almost entirely of students. Their democratic meeting process has gotten better and better over the years. In fact, the day I last visited the meeting was all students. The staff member who was supposed to be there couldn't make it. They take their meeting very seriously.

There are some disadvantages to being just a day school and not having any little kids. But Sands is successful, very strong, and has a very stable staff. Some of the staff and students have participated in the International Democratic Education Conferences from the beginning.

In 1996, the Sands School hosted the IDEC and two Sands students, two girls of about 16 years old, organized it. Before the event I was frustrated because I couldn't find out what was scheduled for that IDEC and I finally called Sean Bellamy, the director of the school, and asked him what was going on. He didn't know because these two students really were organizing the conference themselves.

I eventually discovered that their purpose was to have everybody come to the conference and have the conference co-created on the spot with all the participants, and with particular emphasis on the student input. They felt that to do otherwise would have been to create a typical talking head conference that inevitably would have been adult oriented. It was also designed to last for ten days because they felt the group should become a mini-community instead of coming together for a quick conference and then dispersing.

Their conference, although relatively small, with only about 80 participants, was very successful. It included activities like hiking into the moors, caving, swimming and other things that might not have been scheduled had it been organized entirely by adults. There was also a game there that was being promoted by one of the students called tamborelli, which is sort of a racket game in which you use a tambourine to hit the birdie. And, in fact, there were still the usual talking-head presentations, so it was a diverse mix. It was one of the most interesting conferences I've been to.

Chapter Fifteen
Grownups at School

The meeting process, and democracy itself, is not a science, it's an art. That makes it much more difficult to find a formula to make it work. We can say you have to be very clear about the realm that people are actually making decisions in, and talk about how good a chairperson has to be, but the process has to be one that people accept as a community.

If that doesn't happen, then no matter what you do your process will have problems. At Shaker Mountain we found a lot of it had to do with the makeup of the student body. It was important that we had good student leadership, kids with a lot of experience. Sometimes when we had a whole lot of new students, this would be a problem for a while.

I saw one example of how a school can have problems with this process when I was visiting a boarding school that had a very beautiful campus. They had a democratic process. They even had a beautiful circular room made for the democratic meetings.

The meeting I was invited to observe started out slowly. Announcements were made and then the chairperson asked if it would be possible to give some students a ride to some event they were going to the next night. One of the girls suddenly said, "You know there's been stealing going on in the dormitories." She was very upset about it. Another girl said, "Yes, somebody's been in there. It makes us feel very uncomfortable. We don't know who's doing this. My stuff has been stolen too!"

Then one of the staff members was called on and he said, "Well whoever is doing this is sick, sick! And he has to be caught and chucked out of the school!"

There was about a minute's silence after he spoke and then the chairperson said, "So, can anyone provide transportation for the girls that need to go to this event tomorrow night?"

The chairperson just had no idea how to deal with an emotional issue like this. So finally I raised my hand and was called on and I said, "This kind of thing does go on at boarding schools, at all schools really, and it doesn't necessarily mean that the person is sick. Actually, it might be useful if people let us know who that person is and maybe we can straighten out this problem."

Immediately, the staff member raised his hand and said, "How do you know this person who is stealing is not sick?"

I said, "Well, you don't necessarily know, but this is often the case." After the meeting a number of people came up to me and thanked me for having said what I did. This seemed to indicate that at this school people were having a lot of problems with their meeting process and with trusting the meeting.

This raises a question: how powerful should adults in a democratic community be? The answer depends on the individual community and how strong the kids are in that community. But, properly, in a good community the adults can just be themselves and say what's on their mind and if they're strong people, there will be other strong people in the community who can react to the things they have to say and stand up to them. Ideally you want people to be themselves, to express their ideas and opinions unequivocally. That way you have a better chance to come up with good decisions than if some members of the community hold themselves back for fear of being too powerful.

At democratic schools there are definitely times when adults need to make decisions, especially when health and safety are involved. Because some parents or teachers haven't gone through the process of learning about freedom for themselves, they tend to overreact in the opposite direction and not give their opinions and not put their foot down in a situation where they see something that is just terrible that is going to happen. And then sometimes something terrible does happen.

I had no problems strongly expressing my opinions on issues and so my opinion was always out in the open. We hardly ever had to make some kind of unilateral decision and then only on an individual basis, such as when a kid would go out of control and we would have to grab him till he calmed down. That would happen perhaps once a year.

For a while when we ran two group homes we would sometimes go to meetings of other people who had group homes. They spent an awful lot of time talking about how to physically restrain kids and what to do about kids who ran away. We would just sort of look at each other a little bit flabbergasted because we never had to deal with those situations. The kids didn't run away and almost never had to be physically restrained. This includes the kids who came to us from very bad situations.

It's worth remembering that democratic schools are good for adults, too, but of course that does bring up the fact that most staff members of alternative schools are not products of that system. When you hire a new staff member you just have to hope from what you've seen that the person is going to be able to work through things and have the inherent instincts to listen to kids and interact in a democratic community. But you never know.

The only training for it is to actually do it. I think for some people it doesn't work and they have to go do something different. One surprising thing that I've noticed about intentional communities is that while there is so much emphasis on meeting the needs of the people in the community, they don't usually put a lot of effort and energy into setting up a good alternative school for their kids. Some of them send them to public school, some of them home school them. It has also always surprised me that a group of home schoolers hasn't gotten together to set up an intentional community, and maybe that will still happen.

It's important that the needs of everybody in the school community be met, adults as well as students. Getting too far away from that can create burnout. Burnout happens when the needs of the individual adults in the community are not being met as they focus entirely on the needs of the kids.

One of the problems can be, again, that the adults in the community were not the products of a democratic or alternative school. They may not be good enough at sticking up for themselves and demanding that their own needs be met. It is a potential problem people have to work through, to either learn about or maybe, in some cases, get burned out and get out.

Adults in a community need to understand that a lot of their instincts will be counter to what they're experiencing because of their own experience in school. Even though I have seen amazing things happen with kids in alternative and democratic schools over and over again, they continually surprise me because in my own education I was a product of a traditional system in which these miracles didn't happen.

As I've said, sometimes when you follow your gut, your gut tells you a kid shouldn't have freedom and it won't work. But on the other hand if you suppress the things that you feel, you sometimes are not being genuine.

Then the kids may be missing out on some of the ideas that you have that are important. All you can do is use your best judgment. Again, the more experience that you have with a real functioning democratic community, the more likely you are to make good decisions.

At least there is someone you can trust to make good decisions: the kids! Not only do they make good decisions, they make very effective and creative decisions, often beyond what any of us would have anticipated going into a meeting. I think all of us at Shaker Mountain had confidence in the meeting process, so I would go in there advocating full bore any idea that I thought was good, knowing that nobody was going to accept my idea just because it was mine. They would use any part of it that they thought was useful and build on it or shoot it down if it didn't seem to work.

Democratic process has to evolve over a period of time so that the students and staff come to realize that they must deal with issues as they present themselves. They can't sweep difficult issues under the rug. If they try to do that, these things will come back to haunt them.

Kids' meetings do tend to get to the real bottom of things. I've seen other schools where even though they had a democratic process I felt that adults had a sort of predetermined idea of how decisions were going to come out or should come out. I might go into a meeting with my idea, too, but I knew that the ultimate decision was going to be something other than just my own idea. It was going to be a combination of ideas, and a creative one.

Having democracy for kids implies giving them freedom. In practice, this isn't always true. Many schools have a democratic decision-making process but don't have non-compulsory classes. In most cases this was always a given. From when the school was set up this was not an area in which kids were allowed to make decisions.

It is important to remember that nobody in the world has what you might call absolute freedom. You can have freedom, in relationship to your environment, in varying degrees, but there isn't a single entity called freedom. I can stand there and say to a baby in the playpen, "I now declare you 100 percent free. You can do anything you want. I'm leaving." That won't work.

I've often given the example that you can say to me, "Jerry, I give you permission, you are absolutely free to play Tchaikovsky's violin concerto. I will not stop you. Nobody will stop you." You can even say you will give me the time to do it, the place to do it. That still doesn't mean I'm free to do it. I'll never be free to do that until I have done the work and I have the ability.

These are all aspects of freedom that make it much more complex than people realize. It's a process and a dynamic, rather than something defined and tangible. That's what makes it so tricky and I think it's what makes the word so difficult to define. Any individual freedom will mean different things in different situations. Am I free to live anywhere I want right now? Probably not. Technically, I am. There's nothing that's stopping me from going anyplace I want. Does that mean I don't have the freedom to move or does it mean that I've chosen to stay? Well, you could say I accept the circumstances I'm in and that's the decision that I've made.

With freedom in schools the same is true: the child has to look at the circumstance that he or she is in. For example, you could tell kids in a given alternative school that they are free to use the Internet all day long if they want, but if you only have one computer, their freedom is restricted—they won't individually have the freedom to use the Internet as much as they want.

People look at the issue of children's freedom in too simplistic a way. One of the reasons, of course, is because most adults have not really experienced freedom so they just have a cartoonish idea of what it is. It's subtle and complex and not easily described or defined, and it's always modified by the environment that you're in, the background of the people involved, and so on.

I want to say something more about parents. I think it might be useful for a lot of schools to pay much more attention to parents than they usually do. I've noticed that in some of the schools that we deal with people are beginning to realize they can be more effective with the kids if the parents are more familiar with the philosophy of the school and understand it on a deeper level.

For example, at Grassroots Free School in Florida, Pat Seery requires that any parents who want to send their kids to that school read the book *Summerhill* and see if they agree with it; if they don't, he tells them not to send their kids there. Sharon Caldwell in South Africa has been working a lot with parents to get them to try to understand the basic philosophy of her school. Even though you may not want the parents to be unduly influential, it's still important that the parents be supportive of the school and understand its basic philosophy.

Parents will send kids to an alternative school for many reasons. Sometimes it's out of desperation, and that doesn't necessarily bode well for the school unless the parents actually understand its philosophy.

I wonder if there is any alternative school out there that works as hard with the parents as they do with the kids? Is there any school that actually establishes a program in which the parents grow and develop and learn experientially? I know of no school that does that, but I think it's a good idea.

Chapter Sixteen
A Few Last Words

The power of a children's meeting is in some ways even stronger than the power of our legal system. At Shaker Mountain I remember a situation once in which I got a call from the police who said they had heard that someone was going around collecting donations for a school trip of ours and we told them that was not possible. The only time we ever collected donations was when we went to shopping centers, but we never went door to door.

We didn't think anything more of it. Then a few weeks later I got a letter in the mail with no return address and about a half a dozen checks in it made out to our school all from different people. I thought that was a little strange. So I started calling the people whose telephone numbers were on the checks. They described one or two kids who had come to their door soliciting for Shaker Mountain. After calling enough people, we were able to determine that one of them apparently was the older brother of David, a student at the school. We knew that David's brother had actually spent a little time in reform school. We had David call his brother up and David told me that his brother denied that he had done this.

I got on the phone and said, "It's good that you didn't do it because now we can call the police and give them all the information we have, with the names of the people who wrote the checks, and they can identify the person or persons who did this very easily. If it was you we would probably give you the opportunity to simply come into a school meeting and explain yourself." At that point he decided that maybe he had done it and had done it with one or two of his friends. So the three of them came into a school meeting and were simply raked over the coals by the kids who got them to admit how much cash they had gotten.

What happened, of course, is that they had decided to try to make a little money for themselves by going around and pretending they were collecting for our school and when they got cash that was fine, they could use that. But when they were given checks there was not much they could do with them. One of the kids must have been feeling a little guilty about this and didn't want the money to go to waste, and really did like the school, so he decided to mail the checks to us, not realizing that we could find out who had been doing this. They agreed to pay back the amount of cash that they had gotten and they did so as far as we know. I think facing the school meeting was a tough thing for them to get through.

Sometimes even kids within a community can feel that they are being pushed around by their meeting and being treated unfairly. But for the most part, if the democracy is real, people will feel that the meeting is fair. This is particularly important when it seems like a school is the wrong place for a student, when a kid doesn't have the self-control they need to be able to continue as a part of the community. If a person is eventually asked to leave, they need to realize that the community has done everything it could to keep them there.

When we try to find the key to these schools, we always talk about the democratic process, but the most important thing is the relationship between the adults and the kids and the kind of respect that is shown between the staff and the students. That's why I sometimes give the example of the Stork Family School, which does not specifically have a democratic process but where the students and teachers really respect each other and listen to each other.

I haven't talked about some interesting schools that I haven't visited. There is a school named Moo Ban Dek in a nice location by a river in northern Thailand. It's got about 200 kids, is connected to an orphanage, and was inspired by Summerhill.

There is another school, run by Ram Chandra in Nepal, which is again part of an orphanage. The actual organization is called Sri Aurobindo Yoga Mandir. Sri Aurobindo was an educational pioneer in India and a number of schools are based on his philosophy.

The oldest kids there may be 16 and they take in younger ones all the time. They try to be self-sufficient. They have their own cows, they make incense and sell it, they give yoga classes, they have a woodworking shop, and they have a mill for grain. Lately, the school has been having difficulties because the Maoists have overrun the country and tourism has dried up and their income has gone down 70 percent. I hope that they're going to be able to survive. It seems like the kids are respected and listened to by the staff there, but they don't specifically have a democracy; however, they do seem to be interested in establishing one.

In different parts of the world there are many different ways that schools can be set up legally. For example, we have the classic situation of Summerhill, which is actually owned by the Neill family. As I said before, Zoë Readhead has felt that if it was controlled by a board of trustees they would have caved into public pressure from the English education system a long time ago.

And, as I said, John Potter from the New School of Northern Virginia set up his school as a for-profit that he owned. He was inspired by having spent some time at Summerhill, so he felt this was an important thing. I suggested to him that he set up a non-profit for the purpose of scholarships and they have done that and that's worked well for them, and in fact, Summerhill has just recently done the same thing.

I have seen a lot of serious problems come out of parent cooperatives because sometimes it seems to bring out the worst in the group, almost like setting up a democratic school for adults who have not experienced democracy. These things can become dysfunctional for that reason. That's why I usually encourage somebody who wants to start a school to take responsibility for it themselves and then hopefully they can give that authority back to the community. It really only works well, I think, if you've got a person who believes in the process and is able to do that.

Most of the democratic schools that have been successful over the years have had a strong charismatic democratic leader who was able to empower his or her community. The trouble is there are only a few schools that have made the transition beyond that leadership. You could say one of those is Summerhill, of course, because Neill's daughter Zoë is now running the school. Other examples I have seen are Quaker schools, which seem to be able to continue on after their original leadership, at least so far.

Of course there's The Free School in Albany, now that their founder, Mary Leue, has moved away from the community. There are not a whole lot of examples of this, but hopefully we'll see more as time goes on. I think making that transition is a crucial step, and the process needs a lot more examination.

There is some justification for looking into the possibility of actually franchising something, so that there is a procedure to follow to set up a successful democratic meeting even for a school that doesn't necessarily get founded by such a charismatic leader. It sounds like an oxymoron, like the oxymoron-ish fact that freedom often needs to be very structured to work well. Maybe we should be thinking more about a structure that anybody could follow. Sudbury Valley is already doing this successfully. They are offering people their school-starting kits, and that has been working well.

Maybe we need to look at this in a broader sense. I've thought that there needs to be a charter school organization that can help people who want to do a democratic charter school, something to compete with the for-profit Edison Charter Schools, for example. We can't give up on the charter school idea yet, but of course it has been very much skewed in the direction of being more like a public school than a democratic school. That doesn't mean it's not possible to do these things. We need to put some effort into trying to see if we can.

I've only visited one charter school that was run democratically, and not recently. It certainly was limited by being a public school. They could only hire teachers that were certified. It took a lot of work to get all the parents' signatures and the transportation arranged if they wanted to take a trip, whereas if they were a private alternative it wouldn't have been so difficult. But new and more democratic charters are now starting.

We worked with another charter school down in Florida. Their local school board withdrew support and it evolved into a private school. Blue Mountain in Oregon, which is not a charter school but is public under some other law, seems to be one school that is working democratically and remains a public school. The Village School in Minnesota is a democratic charter. There are several others that call themselves democratic, but I haven't seen them. Trillium, the new school in Portland, Oregon, is trying to be democratic. It's now in the middle of its first year, which is very tough.

The important thing we are working for is for parents and students to have real choice and not to feel trapped into having to go to their local designated school. Options can include everything from Montessori schools, one of the biggest systems, to Waldorf, based on Rudolf Steiner, charter schools, some magnet schools, higher education alternatives, home schooling, public choice and public at-risk alternatives, and of course independent private schools. This wide spectrum is part of the strength of the alternative school movement.

There is no doubt that the movement is growing. Some of the largest areas of growth include the charter schools and home schooling. Many public at-risk alternatives have been created but I have trouble with that particular segment, because a lot of them tend to be somewhat punitive and segregate out this population rather than being learner centered. But it's hard to generalize because you have to look at each individual program carefully to determine whether they are what we call "soft jails" or whether they are more nurturing programs.

One thing is obvious. With the explosive growth of these alternatives, at some time in the future they will no longer be alternative: they will be the mainstream. At that point we may have to come up with another name for them, but nothing else has been able to stick so far. The traditional system has been out of date for a long time and simply maintains itself in a familiar shape out of inertia. Their approach is so out of step with what is needed in the information age that they can't last much longer.

The single most important thing we need is to create a new world in which adults know how to listen to children and to respect them as legitimate human beings. Developing the ability to listen to young people is the key to change.

Printed in the United States
52053LVS00001B/1-33